BABYLON

BY
GARY BARGATZE

Warfield
Happy Hollow
Hurricane Creek
Hollow Rock
McGill
Cabedelo
Thunderwood

For more information about the
Your Winding Daybreak Ways series,
visit the author's website:
www.garybargatze.com

BABYLON

A Human Requiem

GARY BARGATZE

RIGOR HILL PRESS

ISBN-13: 9781545627037

Library of Congress Control Number: 2018902755

Editorial Credit: POP Editorial Services, LLC

Cover Design by Amanda Wright
Interior Design by Agi Bussanich

Printed in the United States of America.

For Elzy, who saved me from a beating

Paths cross beneath October,
Tugging at the sleeve,
Drawing me first into your smile,
And then into a rare love
That whispers, "Carry me to term."

1

PROFESSOR SAMANTHA LYNCH (PSL): "Good morning. You know me as Dr. Lynch; but my partner and close friends call me Sam. That's my post-postmodern way of saying you can call me Sam too. My bio's pretty short. I was born at McGill General some thirty years ago. My father was also born in McGill, attended Pantheon, and has never lost his fascination with technology. He's currently exploring ways to infuse artificial intelligence with empathy and morality. Give the machine a soul, so to speak. My mother was born in the Ivory Coast, studied medicine at Pantheon, presently heads up the psychiatric care unit at McGill General, and owns the contemporary African art gallery in the Thunderwood shopping mall downtown.

"When I reached escape velocity, I moved to Nashville and attended Vanderbilt University following in the footsteps of Brooks, Ransom, Jarrell, and Tate. You see, my dream had always been to become a poet, that is, until plot, character, setting, and theme stepped in the way. So here I am now with eight parts of the whale complete and only one more plus a brief epilogue to go. And thanks to a generous grant, I've traveled from Saint Petersburg, Russia, to Pantheon; become adjunct professor for the academic year; and earned your buy-in to help me finish the tail of this elusive leviathan.

"The idea for this avant-garde approach to creative writing came to me while researching an early-twenty-first-century Russian play, *Flying*, which I had seen in revival while vacationing in the Crimea. From the notes I learned the playwright, Olga Mukhina, had written a verbatim play. That is, she had crafted her work from a series of interviews she had conducted with a dozen or so talented television professionals. While the interviewees provided the bulk of the work—that is, the ideas and dialogue—Ms. Mukhina did the editing and added several stage directions and explanatory notes.

"During your earlier vetting interviews, I explained my goal for our experimental seminar was to assemble a multiracial, multidisciplined, multitalented baker's dozen steeped in literature, the sciences, mathematics, information technology, religion, philosophy, the arts, history, and music who could engage in a free-wheeling discussion of the first eight parts of the whale. As your contracts state, you've agreed to my recording our weekly sessions, my editing the transcripts, and then using your dialogue as the basis for the ninth and final major part of my work, *Your Winding Daybreak Ways*, currently in manuscript stage. In essence you will become a substantial part of the overall work and leave here with a well-deserved A for the course. Oh yes, and before I forget, one minor housekeeping issue. To change things up from time to time, we'll be meeting occasionally over at my rental in the Babylon district, which I've learned the locals here call 'that den of iniquity on the far side of the tracks.' *(student laughter)*

"Are there any questions now before we get started? I see a hand back there. Yes, Thomas?"

FIRST TENOR (FT): "May we ask you questions about your work? I mean if we get bogged down, wander off into a blind alley."

PSL: *(laughs)* "You're sure free to ask, and perhaps on rare occasions I'll respond. We'll start a parking lot up here in the left-hand corner of the board. But keep in mind my primary responsibility is to facilitate, to keep you on track, to ask probing questions that promote analyses and foster insight. And maybe I should emphasize again upfront that my job here is *not* to declare a particular idea right or wrong or to state that I did or didn't have this or that idea in mind while drafting a specific passage. My job is to capture the interaction between you and your colleagues, the interplay between you and the text, and to capture and transform your dialogue into the ninth part of the overall work. Are there any other questions? None? Okay then. Assuming you've finished your precourse reading assignments—that is, all eight completed sections of this whale—please take out your draft copies and let's get started. *(At this point there is a pause and shuffling of papers.)* Everyone ready? Okay then.…"

I flipped the switch on the digital recorder, turned to Professor Rifkin, and said, "As you can see from your transcript there, this is where the analyses begin in earnest. Before we go on, sir, come on back to the guest room with me, and I'll show you the rest of the material."

As the professor entered the bedroom, he exclaimed, "My God, Kyle, there must be fifty boxes in here! Stacked floor to ceiling and wall to wall!"

"That's why I wanted to meet with you here rather than over in your office. I wanted you to see what I had to work with for a PhD thesis. My parents arranged to have all this shipped back from Saint Petersburg where my sister was living. I mean all of it except for a couple of boxes and a laptop, which they retrieved from Sam's rental over in the Babylon district where she was staying while teaching the experimental course, before she disappeared."

"Have you made an inventory of all this?"

"No, not yet. I've sampled a number of the boxes. Mostly early drafts and background material. That's when I found the recordings and thumb drives. The good news is that many of the boxes are labeled and dated, so it shouldn't be too difficult to sort everything out. Do you want to sample a few boxes to get a feel?"

Professor Rifkin shook his head, raised his copy of the transcript, and said, "No, let's go back to your study and continue listening to the recordings. It will help me get a better grip on what we are dealing with here."

Once we were settled back in our respective seats, transcripts in hand, I hit play once again and we listened in silence.

PSL: "In the eighth part, *Thunderwood*, Bones says:

> So we see then great venues demand mighty
> themes, and I might add here, vice versa.
> Melville surely agrees. Earlier in the semester we
> read a passage from *Moby-Dick*: 'No great and
> enduring volume can ever be written on the flea,
> though many there be who have tried it.'

"Before discussing theme, let's start at the ten-thousand-foot level. What genre are we dealing with here in *Your Winding Daybreak Ways*? Who would like to begin? Marie?"

SECOND SOPRANO (SS): "The novel."

PSL: "Can you be more specific? What kind of novel? Anyone?… Yes, there in the back. Patricia"

FIRST ALTO (FA): "I think you tipped us off in *Thunderwood*. In chapter eleven Bones makes the argument:

> The question becomes, "What kind of novel
> are we dealing with when we consider Melville,
> Pynchon, and Powers?" That question demands
> further calibration. I'd call *Moby-Dick*, *Gravity's
> Rainbow,* and *The Gold Bug Variations*

"encyclopedic novels"—voluminous, complex books weaving the arts, the sciences, history, philosophy, theology, and the cultural milieux into the narrative. Like medieval encyclopedists, Melville, Pynchon, and Powers discover, retrieve, and arrange blocks of preexisting narratives and knowledge to help build the frameworks for their cathedrals.

"So I believe Bones's description signals what you are up to in your own work. I believe *Your Winding Daybreak Ways* is an encyclopedic narrative."

PSL: "Anyone else want to add anything about genre before we move on? Okay then. Let's descend a few thousand feet and ask, 'What is the style of *Your Winding Daybreak Ways*?' Who wants to start us off? David?"

SECOND TENOR (ST): "Postmodern."

PSL: "Make your case, David."

ST: "The work is maximalist."

PSL: "Please explain for the non-lit majors."

ST: "*Your Winding Daybreak Ways* embraces over a hundred and fifty years of American history and culture including wars, epidemics, sports, literature, music, politics, race, finance, homosexuality, religion, and technology, for starters."

PSL: "And besides a maximalist approach, what other postmodern characteristics do you see here?"

ST: "There's irony. Playfulness."

PSL: "For example?"

ST: "Well, it's ironic that the most innocent of characters in *Warfield*, a freed slave with the mind of a preteen because of a childhood injury, is hanged for murder by African American Union troops. It's ironic that an autistic, cross-dressing hacker in *Thunderwood* saves the country from years of calamity."

PSL: "And playfulness?"

ST: "Also in *Thunderwood*. The naming and renaming of the 7.0 restaurant through the years, and the process of ordering from the menu, which had been drafted in computer lingo."

PSL: "Other potential postmodern characteristics? Someone else want to jump in? Is that your hand or are you scratching your head, Michael?" *(Good-natured teasing in the professor's voice followed by a ripple of student laughter.)*

THIRD BASS (TB): "Ah, sorry. I believe it's called 'intertextuality'?"

PSL: "Please explain for the rest of us."

TB: "It's incorporating, for example, quotes or story lines from other works. *Your Winding Daybreak Ways* has quotes from the Bible, Dante, Shakespeare, Melville, and Hofstadter to name a few."

PSL: "And you mentioned works based on story lines."

TB: "I believe you can make a credible case that *Cabedelo* is based on the triangular relationship between Brahms and the Schumanns—Samuel Lynch as Brahms, the Squire as Robert Schumann, and Allison as Clara, Robert's wife."

PSL: "Perhaps our music expert can confirm or deny. So what do you think? Does he have a case here, Ann?"

FIRST SOPRANO (FS): "When you add up all the parallels, I think he has a strong case: The Schumanns' daughter answers the door on Brahms's first visit to the Schumann home. Brahms falls deeply in love with Clara, who ultimately rebuffs him because of loyalty to her husband. Robert goes mad, tries to commit suicide, and is hospitalized. Brahms consoles Clara during Robert's madness. Brahms supports the Schumann family financially after Robert's death. Brahms's passion for Clara cools over time but he concedes she is the inspiration for some of his finest works. And the star-crossed lovers continue loving each other from a distance for the rest of their lives." *(brief pause of reflective silence)*

PSL: "Other postmodern characteristics?... Okay. We have another brave soul up front here. Barbara, other characteristics?"

SECOND ALTO (SA): "Fragmentation. The narrative isn't linear. I mean, ah, at least not in the overall work. The timeline jumps around from the distant past to the present and then back again to the recent past."

PSL: "But you seem to be making a distinction between the overall work and the individual sections. Correct?"

SA: "Yes. While *Your Winding Daybreak Ways* is fragmented, the individual parts—for example, *Warfield, Hurricane Creek, Hollow Rock*—these narratives are chronological. Linear."

PSL: "Any other postmodern characteristics? Yes. Over here. Raymond."

FIRST BASS (FB): "In an odd way I think we should also be talking about 'metafiction' in relation to your work."

PSL: "Please define and explain."

FB: "In its simplest terms 'metafiction' is when the author writes about the process of writing. Isn't that what we're doing here? You're capturing our take on the first eight parts of your encyclopedic narrative, which you plan on distilling into a ninth section. So this part here will be about the process of writing. You're turning the first eight sections inside out so the reader can see how the sausage is made. In other words, you're giving them the map for the road to Hana." *(long pause)*

PSL: "Well, it looks like we're about out of time today. Thank you all for your observations. Next session we'll be talking about narrative and setting, so be giving it some thought. Any questions? Okay then, until Wednesday... the gods willing."

2

I SHUT OFF THE RECORDER again and explained, "Bear with me a sec, Professor, I have to find the next lecture. There's a lot of other material on the drive here too."

"No problem, Kyle." Rifkin paused, glanced down at his copy of the transcript, and said, "Forgive me for saying this, but I'm reacting to the recording here on two levels, an intellectual and an emotional one. It's clear that your sister was a great instructor, eliciting objective, insightful responses from her handpicked 'baker's dozen' as she called them. But then, hearing your sister's pleasant, upbeat voice and knowing that she disappeared without a trace... It's chilling."

I nodded. "I know, sir, I have the same response every time I listen to the lectures. And, you know, sir, I haven't dared share these recordings with my parents. They've already been through enough. Hearing Sam's voice after all these years would be devastating for them."

After a reflective pause, I cleared my throat and returned to the task at hand. "I think I've found the second lecture, sir. You ready to continue?"

Rifkin turned the page on his transcript and answered earnestly, "Absolutely! Let's keep going."

Professor Samantha Lynch (PSL): "Good morning. Let's begin with setting; and as time permits, we'll move on to narrative, character, and motif. An easy question to get us warmed up: where does *Your Winding Daybreak Ways* take place? Who wants to start? Okay, go for it, Jane."

THIRD SOPRANO (TS): "Primarily in the western third of Tennessee, with forays into Europe, for example, into Portugal, Denmark, France, and Germany."

PSL: "What about the places in Tennessee?"

TS: "Some are real and some are nowhere to be found. On the one hand you have Nashville, Memphis, Jackson, Humboldt, McEwen—real cities and towns. On the other hand, you have places like Magnolia County, Burnt Bridge, and Grave's Bend, which aren't on any Tennessee maps, old or new."

PSL: "What about the place names we used as titles for the major sections so far, starting with *Warfield*? Is it fact or fiction?"

THE CLASS: "Fiction."

PSL: "*McGill*?"

THE CLASS: "Fiction."

PSL: "*Cabedelo*?"

THE CLASS: "Fact."

PSL: "*Happy Hollow*?"

THE CLASS: "Fact."

PSL: "*Hurricane Creek, Hollow Rock,* and *Thunderwood*?"

THE CLASS: "Fiction, fact, fiction."

PSL: "Very good! And we'll revisit the titles later on. They could be helpful during our analyses of motif. But for now let's move on and dig a bit deeper. Since you've stipulated that the overall narrative is nonlinear and fragmented, how would you describe the cultural and historical context through which the plot lines flow? Fact or fiction? Perhaps we should turn to one of our history experts. So what do you say, fact or fiction, Ted?"

THIRD TENOR (TT): "To be honest with you, I was having a hard time wrapping my head around the narrative because of the fragmentation, so I took the liberty of rearranging the sections chronologically. Everything became much clearer then."

PSL: "So what did you learn about the cultural and historical context?"

TT: It's real. *Your Winding Daybreak Ways* begins with the Civil War. The battles and skirmishes in *Warfield* are well researched, and the local color and lifestyles described are authentic. Then we move on to the yellow fever epidemics in *Happy Hollow*. That neglected story of courage in the face of death is very real. Then it's on to *Hurricane Creek*. Here you seem to take some liberty with the facts. While the description of the political and racial milieu is accurate, the election of the first African American governor is fabricated.

Next we come to *Hollow Rock*, where we know World War I, Prohibition, the birth of the blues, the stock market crash, and World War II were all very real milestones in American history. *(brief pause)* But now it gets a little more complicated."

PSL: "How so?"

TT: "The last three sections become much more subjective. Internalized. But there were some shots across the bow in the earlier parts warning us that we might ultimately be loosed from our objective moorings."

PSL: "For example?"

TT: "Right off the bat in *Warfield* the trail becomes animated through the use of action verbs:

> My axis had always been east-west. My only
> north-south was an abandoned Chickasaw trail
> *bubbling up* miles below Shiloh, *snaking over* the
> Duck River, and *blurring* in a thicket of black-
> berry vine, long before reaching the Dark and
> Bloody Hunting Ground.

"Next, at the end of that first chapter we encounter the milk glass murmurs:

> As the king's wall served centuries before, the
> milk glass centerpiece with crepe around its neck
> became an oracle, both ominous and arcing....
> But we only saw the sunlit splendor; we never
> heard the milk glass murmurs: "Grave's Bend...

Robert… Burnt Bridge… Mama… Fort Pillow…
Rachel… Israel."

"And then we have Master Hudson's recurring dream of a 'blighted landscape where the trees and large brush are cropped and stripped bare of bark'; of 'frozen emerald lakes, where motionless bodies stand suspended in glowing layers of jade'; and of 'a unique cross standing near the entrance to an enormous tent.'"

PSL: "These examples are all in *Warfield*. But do you find these 'shots across the bow,' as you call them, in any of the other early sections?"

TT: "Yes. The dreamlike sequence in *Hollow Rock* when Todd visits the hallowed Indian grounds surrounding the mysterious rock. That would be one example:

> The fog worked its magic, unmooring me from my sense of time and place. The west wind whistled through the glazed woods, lifting the veil on the far-off past. While braves scoured the forest for charred but living trees, the squaws prepared a pit for this "thunderwood," which would soon fuel the sacred fire within the sacred circle. Three long wails. The deep vibration of drums and the rattle of gourds. The swaying of men and trees. Silent prayers to the Thunder Beings and then the whoops of renewal and redemptive joy.

PSL: "And this subjectivism you've pointed out is characteristic of what style?"

TT: "Postmodernism."

PSL: "Yes, another characteristic to be added to our previous discussion of the postmodern style." *(brief pause)* "Now you said the last three sections of the overall work become much more subjective. Internalized."

TT: "Yes, the cultural and historical context takes a backseat to the inner workings of people's minds. I mean, the context and history are still there, but they're deflected, much more diffused. What we learn about historical events we learn tangentially. Our world is now primarily limited to McGill and Pantheon University. What's happening internally is far more important now than what's happening in the state, the country, or the world."

PSL: "Which brings us to the characters. So in the time we have remaining today let's talk about the narrators. By the way, how many narrators are there?… Anyone?… Okay. There's a quick hand. Robert."

SECOND BASS (SB): "Seven!"

PSL: "How many?"

SB: "Ah, seven?" *(Speaker's confidence is eroding.)*

PSL: "Anyone else want to take a shot? Yes. Over there. Diane."

THIRD ALTO (TA): "I believe there are six."

PSL: "Can you name them for us?"

TA: "Let's see.... There's Thomas. He's the narrator in *Warfield* and *Happy Hollow*. Then there are Todd, Andrew, Jason, Lil Jim, and Samuel."

PSL: "How many of you agree there are six narrators? Raise your hands. Looks like there's a consensus here. Let the record show there are thirteen hands raised." *(another brief pause)* "But you'll have to forgive me. It's something of a trick question. You've named six, but I have to respect-fully disagree." *(A door opens. There are footsteps and whispers. After a pause the professor continues.)* "I apologize, I have to attend to a medical emergency off campus. We'll have to stop here today and pick up where we left off next Monday… the gods willing."

3

WHEN I STOPPED THE recorder again to find the next lecture, Professor Rifkin jumped in. "Any idea what was going on there? I mean with the emergency off campus?"

I shook my head. "No. Not really. When I first heard the recording, I thought that Sam might have been talking about our mother's car crash that happened around the same time. But after conducting a little research at home, I discovered that the off-campus emergency and our mother's accident were off by a little over a week. So the mystery stands. I just don't know." I pointed to the digital recorder and asked, "You ready for the next lecture?"

"Yes, indeed, let's go on," the professor replied. He then lowered his voice and mumbled, "Yes, indeed...."

Professor Samantha Lynch (PSL): "Good morning. Good to see you again after a week away." *(brief pause)* "Now that we've touched a bit on genre, style, narrative, and character, let's delve into that provocative world of motif and theme.

To ensure we're all on the same page, I would like one of our literature majors to help us out with definitions. These terms can get confusing. Do I see a hand? Okay, Michael. Please define *theme* for us."

TB: "Theme is the primary idea or message of a literary work."

PSL: "And how does that differ from motif?"

TB: "Motif is a recurring idea or object that can be used to help develop a theme."

PSL: "Thank you, Michael. So let's start with motif and work our way up to theme. Questions to keep in mind now: Are there separate motifs and themes for each of the major parts so far? Or do we find a consistency of motif and theme throughout the entire work?... Who would like to offer up the first of the motifs? I think we have a bidder there. Okay, Ted. Go for it!"

TT: "I believe 'ill treatment of the oppressed and the underclass' is a major motif that runs through all major parts of *Your Winding Daybreak Ways* and helps inform the overall theme."

PSL: "Some examples, please."

TT: "As I said earlier, I had trouble with the fragmentation, so I want to go at this chronologically, if you don't mind."

PSL: "No harm, no foul."

TT: "The first mention of the oppressed or underclass occurs obliquely in the first paragraph of *Warfield*, which we've already quoted in our discussion of subjectivism: 'My only north-south was an abandoned Chickasaw trail bubbling up miles below Shiloh.' In this context the key word is 'abandoned,' indicating something might have happened to these 'Spartans of the lower Mississippi Valley' who traveled the path northward to hunt in Kentucky. Why would they abandon such an important trail, one that was key to the tribe's survival?

"And then we discover that something has indeed happened to this proud people who had settled the land during the Middle Ages, who later drove the French from the territory, who frustrated Spanish ambition, and even defeated Americans in the Revolutionary War. We read that after many negotiations, treaties, and official acts of Congress, all the Chickasaw lands had been wrested from the tribe by the 1830s. So about five thousand Chickasaws were forced to pull up stakes and migrate westward to southeast Oklahoma.

"But that was only the beginning of the suffering for Native Americans. Next came the Indian Wars, followed by the US government's brutal 'mopping up' missions. For example, in *Hurricane Creek* we learn that because of a congressional deportation act in the 1890s, Pershing and his African American troopers were tasked with transporting a 'motley collection' of Cree—families, horses, livestock, and personal possessions—a hundred and fifty miles northward to Coutts Station in Alberta, Canada. This particular 'trail of tears' featured an unceremonious ride to the Canadian border in filthy, crowded cattle cars."

PSL: "Other examples of ill treatment of the oppressed and the underclass? Okay, David."

ST: "African Americans who came to this country as slaves and powered the South's economic engine. They were an invaluable commodity with very little monetary value."

PSL: "Please explain."

ST: "In *Happy Hollow* we learn that Thomas's grandmother had inherited two slaves along with two hundred acres of real estate from her brother, who had died prematurely of a fever. The brother's last will had valued the land at two thousand dollars and the slaves, Bella and Israel, at fourteen hundred dollars together. So the two slaves combined had less *worth* than the farm and timberland. But they were an extremely valuable commodity. This is something Lincoln understood about our people and slavery. If he freed the slaves through the Emancipation Proclamation, he would disrupt the South's primary source of revenue for financing the war—its agriculture. And on top of that he would also have a fresh supply of soldiers fighting for the Union cause."

PSL: "A slightly cynical reading of Lincoln's motives, don't you think?"

ST: "Not really. As a history major, I've done some in-depth analyses of the run-up to the emancipation. And Lincoln's use of the proclamation as part of a military strategy isn't even half the surprises that greeted me along the way. Lincoln didn't even believe we should have equal rights with white folk. In his senatorial debates with Stephen Douglas, Lincoln denied supporting racial equality. He said, 'I will say then that I am not, nor ever have been, in favor of bringing about in any way the social and political equality of the white and black races.' He then went on to fully stake out his position that African Americans shouldn't have the right to serve on juries, to vote, or to hold office. In fact, he was all for solving the slavery issue through colonization—sending all of us either to Central America or back to West Africa.

"And then after the emancipation our young black men flocked to the Union army, fought bravely throughout the South, and suffered immeasurably at Nashville and Fort Pillow. For what? The few years of Reconstruction and suffrage we enjoyed before the southern elites realized their voting majority was disappearing before their eyes? Realized that without a majority, there would be no Redemption, no returning to the old ways of the antebellum South? And how did the elites regain control? That's the story you've told in *Hurricane Creek*—through voter suppression, the Klan, biased editorials to stir rebellion, intimidation, assault, destruction of property, and even murder. And the elites did all this after the horrific yellow fever epidemics had preyed on them and we black folk had stayed behind to protect their houses, care for their sick, and bury their dead."

PSL: *(After a long, reflective pause with classroom murmuring in the background.)* "Thank you, David, for your insights. Someone else now. Did African Americans make further contributions to the country's westward expansion? To its 'manifest destiny'? All right, Diane."

TA: "Yes, Ms. Lynch… ah, Sam. They made significant contributions. Our black ancestors did much of the heavy lifting during the Indian Wars, fighting the Cheyenne, the

Comanche, and the Apache off and on for almost thirty years. But in *Hurricane Creek* we learn the thanks they got when they mustered back East before shipping out to fight in the Spanish-American War." *(Shuffling of papers before beginning to read.)*

> The next six weeks in May and June of '98 were filled with tension—not so much from the anticipation of going to war but from the reception we received from the local citizenry. My soldiers had been out West for years, enjoyed many victories and gained genuine respect from soldier and civilian alike. So when we shipped out to Florida, we expected to be treated as we had been in the past; we weren't prepared for the discrimination and bigotry we faced day in and day out.

PSL: "And how did the African American troopers perform in the Spanish-American War?"

TA: "Without question they fought superbly. In fact, they saved Teddy Roosevelt's bacon at least twice during the war, once at Las Guásimas and then again on San Juan Hill. And what thanks did the black troopers get this time? Again, as we learn in *Hurricane Creek*, they were cropped out of the famous photograph taken atop San Juan Hill after the battle had ended."

PSL: "And what happened when the troopers returned home to their families?"

TA: "After the Spanish-American War faded into the history books, the country returned to business as usual. The black troopers returned to their second-class citizenship, to discrimination, neglect, and too often to abuse. And as we read in *Hollow Rock*, the pattern repeats itself again and again—in World War I and then again in World War II. The black soldiers fight and die for love of country and return home again to discrimination, neglect, abuse, murder, and lynching. The highly decorated black veteran, Jesse Lockwood, suffers such a fate after World War II:

> When the argument escalated, the driver called the police. And when the local sheriff arrived, the driver asked the lawmen to arrest Jesse for public drunkenness. Jesse objected vehemently to the charge, explaining he was a minister and a teetotaler. When the sheriff tried handcuffing him, Jesse spontaneously pushed away, infuriating the officer. The sheriff reached for his billy club and beat Jesse mercilessly. He then threw the unconscious war hero in the back of his cruiser and hauled him off to jail. The next morning, the sheriff dragged Jesse before a corrupt judge who found Jesse guilty and fined him a hundred dollars plus court costs. After his rigged prosecution that morning, Jesse stumbled out of the courthouse and collapsed in the street. The curb became his stone of destiny.

PSL: "Thank you, Diane. So far we've discussed Native and African Americans. Do you see any other depiction of the oppressed or underclass in *Your Winding Daybreak Ways*? Anyone?... Okay, Patricia."

FA: "I can think of two additional groups who despite living in the shadows made significant contributions to society."

PSL: "The first?"

FA: "The prostitutes in *Happy Hollow* who stayed behind in Memphis to care for the sick and dying during the yellow fever epidemics. We read that one of the madams even became known as the 'Mary Magdalene of Memphis.'"

PSL: "And the second group of underclass and oppressed?"

FA: "Gays. First, the gay professors in *McGill*, Walter Talley and Donald Sanders, who felt compelled to hide their love. And second, in *Hurricane Creek*, the gay entrepreneur and politician, Hurricane Jim Taylor, who knew his business and political careers would have ended abruptly if he had revealed his orientation to the public."

PSL: "Thank you, Patricia. Any other groups of the oppressed or underclass you see depicted here in *Your Winding Daybreak Ways*?... Jane."

TS: "The main characters in *Thunderwood* who perfect a software that saves the national grid. They all appear to have differences that cause 'neurotypicals' to continually ostracize them."

PSL: "Excellent. Any other groups?... Going once... twice. Okay, then. So in the overall work we find a number of the underclass and the oppressed—Native Americans, African Americans, gays, prostitutes, and people with developmental differences. Question: did all the groups here contribute positively to society?"

THE CLASS: "Yes."

PSL: "Is it possible then that the real motif is lurking somewhere below the surface here? If it's not the ill treatment of the oppressed and the underclass, what else could it be?… Anyone? No? How about a clue? Zulu's theory.… Anyone? Okay, Marie."

SS: "In *Thunderwood* Zulu rightly believes there is a second genome hidden below the first. The top layer of code expressing proteins as deciphered in the 1960s, a second layer controlling gene switching."

PSL: "But how does her theory relate to the oppressed and the underclass?"

SS: "Ahh, I see now. They're that second hidden layer of society that rarely gets credit for anything—like settling the lands, winning the wars, curing the sick, and crafting literature and poetry."

PSL: "Ah, which reminds me. Since we have a few minutes remaining and it's our last class before the Thanksgiving break, let's check the questions you've posed after class, which we've steered into the parking lot here on the board. Question number one: Why choose to use a pseudonym and why this particular Polish name?" *(The professor writes on the board.)* "Answer: So there you have a list arguably of six major encyclopedic novelists. What do they all have in common?… Barbara."

SA: "Gender."

PSL: "Thank you. And why this pseudonym? Answer: Chance, pure and simple. The name cropped up while I was researching the science angle for *Thunderwood*, first in relation to cell-cell communications and then in conjunction with solar winds. Having the name pop up twice in two very different fields of scientific research piqued my interest. And with a little digging I discovered it's not a Polish name after all but based on an Italian saint who converted to Christianity and was beheaded at fourteen in AD 304. By the way, the name in Greek means 'the one that holds everything,' which fits nicely as the pen name for an encyclopedic novelist, don't you think?" *(Laughter ripples through the room.)*

"Question number two: Is *Your Winding Daybreak Ways* biographical in any way? Answer: No, it's not biographical.

"Question number three: Why do you plan on calling this current part of your overall work *Babylon: A Human Requiem*? Is it because it's the district where you are currently living? Answer: To some degree I had the district in mind, but more importantly it's the biblical site where God became a co-conspirator. And as far as the requiem? Simply paying homage to Brahms.

"And question number four: In *Thunderwood* Jason says the dedication to Richard Fariña is a good way to 'pick the lock' in *Gravity's Rainbow*. What would you say is a good way to 'pick the lock' when it comes to *Your Winding Daybreak*

Ways? Answer: To circle that square I would say the sixth section, *McGill*, and the eighth section, *Thunderwood*." *(A murmur spreads throughout the room.)* "Well, I see our time is up for today. So after the holiday break, we will continue analyzing motifs, which will ultimately lead us to an overarching theme. That is, the gods willing."

4

I FLIPPED THE SWITCH ON the digital recorder and turned to Professor Rifkin. "That's where the recordings end, Professor. So do you want to go back to the guest room now and sample a few of the boxes to get a better feel of the overall material?"

"No, that won't be necessary, Kyle. I think I have a fairly clear picture of what you have here. Let's go sit down and discuss your proposal."

"Could I interest you in a glass of Napa Valley cab while we talk?"

"That would be really great. Thanks, Kyle."

I stepped into the kitchen to retrieve the wine bottle. I was anxious to hear the professor's verdict, so I rushed back with the wine, offered a brief, forgettable toast, and got right down to business. "So what do you think of my proposal, Professor?"

"Well, after listening to the recordings and seeing the amount of material that you have stored in the back room there, I think editing your sister's unfinished work for a doctoral thesis is an exciting idea."

"It's a go then?"

"Sure is. I look forward to advising you on your sister's work."

"Thanks so much, sir. That's a real relief."

"Well, let's get started then. So in your proposal you say you have seven completed novel-length manuscripts. Correct?"

"Yes. I have digital and hard copies. Approximately a half million words all told. They are each pretty much self-contained. I believe you could publish each of the seven parts individually as full-blown novels."

"How much of the ninth part, *Babylon*, do you have?"

"The recordings, some notes Sam made during the class, outlines. There's enough material here to get an idea where she was going with it."

"So are we dealing with Schubert's Eighth or Mahler's Tenth?"

"More on the scale of Mahler's Tenth. I have a decent grip on the narrative arc."

"So the plan is to edit the seven novel-length sections with endnotes; include a transcript of the recordings and any relevant notes for the current part, *Babylon*; and write an introduction discussing everything in detail. Correct?"

"That's right, sir."

The professor stood up and extended his hand, signaling our meeting was at an end. "Sounds like a plan, Kyle."

"Thank you, sir. Here, I'll take the glass and get your coat. Looks like a blizzard out there."

Just as I opened the front door to let the professor out, Jennifer stepped into the room. "We've been standing here waiting for you, Jenn," I joked. "Where have you been?"

"Trudging through knee-deep drifts all the way from the studio," she said, as she brushed the snow off the shoulders of her peacoat. "It's a mess out there."

I turned to the professor and said, "I'd like you to meet my fiancée, Jennifer Townsend, our resident sculptress, who is finishing her fine arts doctorate here at Pantheon. And Jenn, this is Doctor Jack Rifkin, my thesis adviser."

Jennifer extended her hand and said, "Good to meet you, sir. Kyle has had a lot of nice things to say about you."

"Nice to meet you too, Jennifer," Professor Rifkin replied. "And would I be right in saying that I've seen some of your sculptures at the galleries around town?"

"Yes, sir. From time to time they feature my pieces."

"Well, now that we've met, I'll sure keep an eye out for your sculptures when I visit the galleries. I'm always on the lookout for new, exciting works of art."

Jennifer smiled broadly and responded with a wink, "This starving artist certainly thanks you, sir."

The professor laughed and replied, "No problem, Jennifer. I'll certainly keep you in mind." He then paused; and as he finished buttoning his overcoat, he said, "I hate to rush off now, but with the way the snow's coming down, I don't want to pull a Whittier."

Jennifer laughed, looked over at me, and teased, "*A Snow-Bound* joke. I like him already." She turned back to the professor and said, "But seriously, sir, watch those front steps. They're a sheet of ice. You could really go skating."

"Believe me, the handrail will be my friend all the way down. And Kyle, check in sometime toward the latter part of next week and let me know how you're making out with the research."

"Yes, sir. Most likely Thursday, since I have a couple of undergraduate classes to teach on Wednesday."

"No problem. See you then."

We followed the professor out onto the porch and repeated our warnings as he cautiously descended the stairs and finally disappeared into the swirling January snow.

5

Jennifer dropped a stack of manila folders on the coffee table, curled up on the couch, and said, "Well, I've got all my notes here. So where do you want to begin?"

"Why don't we pick up where Sam left off, analyzing the motifs. She had only gotten through the one, and I know of at least two or three other major ones."

"You want me to start off then?" she asked.

"Why not? And I'll do the honors capturing all our ideas on the flip chart here."

"Okay, then. Here goes. Motif number two: loss. After Thomas loses his father early on in *Warfield*, the losses just keep piling up. He loses his first love, Beth. Then his sister, Rachel, loses her lover, Burns. Bella loses Israel. The community loses Miss Owings and five schoolchildren in a fire. And near the end of *Warfield* Thomas sums up all the losses and says, 'Repeating their names now was the forlorn sound of the successive nails piercing Father's coffin.'"

"And don't forget all the references to past losses," I added. "The Greek epidemics, Wallace, Leonidas and the 300, and

Wordsworth's little Lucy Gray, not to mention the Civil War, which was raging all around Thomas and his family."

Jennifer nodded and said, "Yes, and the next section chronologically, *Happy Hollow*, is all about loss during the yellow fever epidemics of the 1870s. Thomas paints a bleak picture of Memphis. Should I read one of my favorite passages aloud?"

I smiled and replied, "Sure. Why not?"

"It's when Hannah and Thomas enter the infected zone for the first time." Jennifer paused, scanned her copy of the manuscript, and then began to read in a soft but dramatic tone:

> The following morning Hannah and I pierced the thick, black veil of the fever fires and entered hell. A stifling, deathly silence now trumped the sunrise sounds of wagons we'd heard only seconds before. Taste and smell merged into a single sense, heightening the nausea from the unbearable stench of vomit, musk, decay, and cologne. Smoldering heaps of infected mattresses bathed the inferno in a callous gray. Our boots were white with disinfectant. It was hot, and stacks of coffins stood at the corners awaiting Undertaker Jack. Every window of every house was nailed shut against the scourge—some with yellow placards signaling the fever and many with superfluous black cards requesting caskets for the dying and the dead. Superfluous because

layers of flies already lined the outside walls, forecasting or announcing death with a whir-ring as foreboding as that of swarming bees.

"And along with the deaths came the anguish of loss." Jennifer paused again, thumbed quickly through her *Happy Hollow* manuscript until she reached the last page, and then continued. "As he had done at the end of *Warfield*, Thomas also reflects here on the loss of family and friends:

> I moved through the main gate and passed the heroes' trench where thousands of caskets lay buried side by side and end to end—ministers, priests, nuns, and nurses among them—vol-unteers who'd come to help and landed here. I found the Taylor plot, hitched the mare, and walked over to the graves. I stood facing the markers and waited. And right on cue, the bell began tolling. After each of the four peals, I repeated the name etched on the headstone— Emma… Preston… Amanda… Hannah.

I quickly scrawled our observations on the flip chart, then eased in again. "Don't forget the references to past calami-ties here too. The plagues of Athens and Constantinople, the pestilence of Florence, the Great Plague of Milan, and the epidemic of Defoe's seventeenth-century London."

"Agreed," Jennifer said. "But with *Hurricane Creek*, your sister pivots. While the characters continue suffering losses, it's no longer so much about loved ones dying as it is loss because of other circumstances. Lil' Jim says, 'When my uncle moved us back to Memphis, the children stopped coming by to play. I was going on seven, and it was the first time I had ever felt loneliness.' Lil' Jim attributes his loss to race:

> As the birthdays passed, I became more iso-
> lated. I became a stranger in a familiar land. I
> increasingly realized I could go where my family
> couldn't. I could walk uptown to the markets
> without causing a stir. The white folk were none
> too friendly, but that was because I was young
> and nameless. It had nothing to do with my
> appearance. You see, unlike the rest of my family,
> my physical features and skin color resembled a
> white male in every way. But unfortunately, my
> looks cut two ways. I no longer felt comfort-
> able at school, at home, or in South Memphis.
> It wasn't so much a reaction to hostility. It was
> more a feeling of neglect and always being the
> odd man out.

"And when Lil' Jim runs away at sixteen on Christmas Eve, he ends up in a no-man's-land with a motley crew of 'sojourners' who blame their losses on bad luck. These hobos— 'the old, the young, the sinner, the saint, the playwright, the poet, the hustler, and the priest'—are all dreamers with an unshakable belief that their luck will change."

"That's a good point, Jenn. The motif of loss impacts the minor characters here just as it does in *Moby-Dick*.... But then it's back to race as a factor for loss in *Hollow Rock*. Todd's good friend, Jesse Lockwood, explains that when he and his mother moved back to his grandparents' place, he spent a lot of time alone because 'the white folk… didn't take too kindly to my color and warned their children to stay away from me and our farm.'"

Jennifer interrupted. "Yes, and don't forget Todd's loss too. He suffers the breakup of his family because of his father's homosexuality."

I eased in again. "And speaking of Todd's father, Hurricane Jim loses his bid for reelection not because of his divorce, remarriage, or homosexuality but because of Uncle Aaron's diary, which reveals Hurricane Jim does indeed have 'Negro blood coursing through his veins.'"

Our ideas continued feeding off each other as Jennifer jumped back in. "Todd loses his 'mother'/lover, Van, because of their age disparity and must accept Van's daughter, Catarina, as a disappointing, unsatisfying second prize."

"And Todd loses a fortune in the '29 crash. And later he loses a leg in the Second World War." I paused, flipped through my notes on the table, and said, "You know, Jenn, I think we've got enough examples here to support our assertion about loss. So you ready to move on to a third motif?"

"Sure. Have at it!"

"Well, I would paint this major motif with a broad brush as 'existentialism' and include here the ideas of loneliness and isolation and the images of a balance scale and a pendulum. You okay with 'existentialism' as an umbrella label?"

Jennifer smiled and replied, "Yeah, that works for me. Would you like me to do the honors?"

"Go for it!" I said.

"Back to the first section, *Warfield*, again?"

"Yes, back to *Warfield* for a second circling of the square."

"Okay, here goes. In the opening paragraphs the narrator, Thomas, introduces the balance scale:

> I recall Master Hudson mounting his one-room stage and speaking to us in pictures: "All right boys and girls, stand up; put your arms out straight from your sides—straight like the highway out front. Turn your hands palms up and cup 'em. You're now a balance scale. Your body is the fulcrum, your outstretched arms make the beam, and your palms are the weighing pans."

"But by the end of this initial scene, the mood has darkened and the schoolchildren have somehow arced from youthful innocence to existential nothingness:

> Reflecting now on that schoolhouse scene and knowing all that has happened since, innocents

stand there with their arms outstretched echoing the biblical Peter, Andrew, and even Christ himself at the Place of the Skull. Young martyrs living a human arc from oblivion to innocence, from joy to anxiety, from fear to horror and then back again to nothingness.

"And it's not long before Thomas begins offering explanations for how 'innocence' could ever arc to 'nothingness.' He introduces the battlefield imagery: 'The day Beauregard signaled at Sumter was the day the gods declared war on us.' So Thomas now suspects the gods play a deliberate and decisive role in death and human suffering."

I rushed in excitedly. "Yes, which drives the main characters in *Warfield* to ask the existential question, 'why?' Thomas loses his first love, Beth, and using the balance scale imagery again, says:

But then Beth came along, and everything changed. The balance beam began moving in my favor. But no, the thumb couldn't allow too much pleasure or happiness here. Pain is its realm; suffering its purview. So, it's now sliding away, sliding back toward Robert. And the supplicant here has been reduced to thrusting his arms into the air and assertively asking, 'Why?'

"And after the black troops execute her only son, Bella asks the existential question: 'Why, Jesus? Why?' Then, following Mama's funeral, Thomas and Master Hudson sit on the front porch and stretch 'why?' to the breaking point. Master Hudson offers a probing soliloquy:

> I thought Reverend Lyons gave a good sermon today, praising all the caring acts your mama'd done for everyone over the years. But he sure didn't answer our 'why?' question, did he, Thomas?…

> You and I started out talking about Moses, the Massacre of the Innocents, Caledonia, the Napoleonic Wars, and asking ourselves, 'Why would a loving God allow such cruelty, dissembling, and human suffering?' But over the last few years, it's become personal for you and me: your grandfather, your father, your mother, your brother, Israel, my mama, Miss Owings, the five innocents at the schoolhouse… Got me to thinking. Maybe we should push beyond 'why?' to 'what if?'

> We've always assumed there was a capricious puppeteer controlling the strings behind the curtain, but what if we stepped behind the screen and saw there wasn't anyone there?… I wonder,

would that be more frightening than believing there are gods who sometimes bless us while reserving the right to destroy us at any time?

By pushing past Dante and Shakespeare to 'why did the gods allow these things to happen?' we've excused the marionettes' actions because we're blaming their masters, the puppeteers. In our carnival we've accepted the shocking, the absurd, the outrageous. We've permitted the puppets to say and do almost anything they've wanted to, just because we've stipulated it's not their fault. Since the supreme puppeteers control the marionettes, we exonerate our human puppets, granting them absolution.

But ya know, Thomas, in a perverse reading of Shakespeare, Cassius could be right: 'The fault, dear Brutus, is not in the stars, but in ourselves.' Perhaps our hell never really had anything to do with the heavens or the gods, just chance and inhumanity. And if this were true, then how can we make life tolerable? How can we face this unpredictability and human cruelty?... As we discussed during one of my early visits, it's strange how the source of our suffering might just be our path to salvation. We have each other.

After a long, reflective pause, Jennifer asked, "You ready for the next part of the narrative, *Happy Hollow*?"

"Yes, on to *Happy Hollow*."

She thumbed through her notes briefly and said, "I guess we should start with the opening lines where Thomas returns to the battlefield imagery foreshadowing what's to come:

> As the guns fell silent at Appomattox the gods were already shaping the next battlefield. None of us realized the target would be narrowed this time to just eight square miles overlooking the Mississippi. We each believed we had our own reasons for leaving our homes and settling on the bluffs.… And then again later on we had our own reasons for staying once the ungodly attacks began in earnest: blind faith, a sense of duty, and an unfathomable willingness to race toward death as the masses fled in panic.

"And it's not long before Memphis begins feeling the gods' wrath. During a family gathering, Master Taylor informs his household that the steam-tug *Bee* had dropped a dying deck hand off at Happy Hollow and then returned to Memphis the following day from Osceola with the body of the *Bee*'s captain. When he adds that some of the folks in Happy Hollow had now shown signs of illness, Mrs. Taylor interrupts, describing a recurring nightmare she had had where stacks of coffins are loaded into the back of hearses and carried off to the cemeteries day in and day out. Master Taylor responds with reassurances that most likely the current sickness wouldn't spread to other parts of the city. Thomas, who has already experienced the horrors of *Warfield*, thinks to himself: 'I'm sure the gods smiled at his reassurances; they relish proving us wrong.'"

"Very good analysis, Jenn," I said, as I flipped to a new page on our chart and eased back into the conversation. "And this doubting Thomas, if you will, keeps on questioning. When the Memphis Madam, Miss Cook, converts her brothel to a hospital a second time and contracts the deadly yellow fever herself, Thomas helps care for this 'Mary Magdalene of Memphis.' He describes her painful last days with a graphic description of hemorrhaging, convulsions, kidney failure, and projectile vomiting.

"And he follows that up with an existential observation harboring a troubling but unspoken 'why?': 'As I lay in the dark at the edge of sleep, a blasphemous notion crossed my mind: Miss Cook had suffered unspeakably for six days while Jesus endured only six hours on the cross to save the world.'"

Jennifer referred to her notes and said, "And in *Hurricane Creek*, a dying soldier also raises thorny existential issues. Remember, Kyle?"

"Yes, of course. But lay it out so that I can capture it on the chart here."

"Okay then. So First Sergeant Blair and Hurricane Jim stumble on a gravely wounded Buffalo soldier who has been dumped in the thicket by the medical team and left to die.

They sit down beside the African American warrior, waiting for his life to ease away. As he holds the dying soldier's hand, Hurricane Jim asks Blair: 'Don't you imagine, Sergeant, this fellow prayed to make it out of here alive, to head home and pick up where he'd left off?' The sergeant then introduces the existential 'why?' with his answer:

> Looks like no one was listening to him up there today, Hurricane. You know, I've always wondered about that—why they hear one appeal and not another. We were all praying this morning before we charged the trenches, that's for damn sure. So you and I are here healthy and he's lying there swallowing his own blood. Why'd they hear us and not him?... And then again tomorrow they might not hear you or me. Ever think about that, Hurricane?

I eased in again and said, "And then the questions keep on coming in the final parts of *Your Winding Daybreak Ways*, don't they, Jenn?"

She nodded and then asked, "You ready for *Cabedelo*?"

"Yes. Let's move on to *Cabedelo* and capture a few final points."

"Well, here goes. The narrator, Samuel, opens the crucial tenth chapter with an ominous, existential foreshadowing of the Squire's downward spiral into madness after his young daughter's inexplicable death. Samuel writes:

The gods always seem to know where to find the loose threads that unravel the soul. Despite their unbearable loss, Allison and the Squire managed to maintain their composure throughout the obligatory ordeal of the viewing, the funeral, and the twilight burial near Grandma in the Afterlife cemetery.

"Yes," I said, "and then Samuel focuses on Reverend Williams's valiant attempt at using the scriptures to address the thorniest of existential issues—'why do the gods tear our children from us?' Samuel describes his impression of the reverend's eulogy for little Carolina, ending with the observation, 'He had failed to tackle his own highly visible initial question, "why?," which we all wanted answered with devout conviction.'"

After another long pause, Jennifer whispered, "Your sister is really probing the depths here, isn't she, Kyle?"

I nodded and replied, "Yes, and you know, Jenn, in some ways Sam's work reminds me of your sculptures."

She leaned in and probed, "So how's that, Kyle?"

"Oh, the expression on the faces of some of your figures. Take, for example, your latest work, 'Wanderers,' where we see the grimacing, the clenched teeth, the eyes focused on the heavens, as if the man and woman there, as if all humanity is asking, 'why?'"

She gazed into my eyes and said, "That's one of the things I really love about you, Kyle: your ability to interpret my works, to read my soul."

I smiled, capped the marker in my hand, and muttered the Moonspell lyric from Professor's Morton's "immortal lecture" in *Thunderwood*:

> Why is everything to be denied?
> That could make life a little bright.

6

I SET THE DANISH AND espressos on the end table
and asked, "You ready to get started?"

Jennifer shook her head slowly and replied, "No. Not just
yet. Something's gnawing at me."

"What's up, Jenn?"

"I got to thinking about that last motif, existentialism.
Well, let's see.... How to explain? The balance scale, the pendulum, the oscillations from dark to light and back again—
it's as if your sister's writing reflects her feelings in real time.
I mean, what she was experiencing, sensing, as she wrote. I
don't know for sure, but something in my gut says we ought
to pursue the biography as much as the text, especially while
conducting the interviews. I realize you know little to nothing
of your sister's life and whereabouts after she left home for
college. After all, you were an infant and her relationship
with your parents was somewhat strained. But I think it's
worth a shot. Who knows what we might turn up that could
give you a better insight while editing her work. The connection might seem tenuous, but there's one existential passage
in particular that pushed me over the edge."

"What's that?"

"In *Cabedelo*, Samuel—or is it your sister, Sam?—describes the fabled heavyweight championship fight between Dempsey and Georges Carpentier of France. She writes:

> In summary, it was David versus Goliath and for just eleven seconds of the second round the crowd felt they were witnessing a miracle. Carpentier nailed Dempsey with a straight right hand, which caught the champion flush on the jaw. Dempsey rocked back, then forward, and his arms dropped helplessly at his side. For a brief moment the champ was vulnerable; and Carpentier swung a powerful right-hand uppercut that missed.… The champ held on until he regained his senses and then stayed close to Carpentier the rest of the fight. In the next two rounds, Dempsey wore the brave Frenchman down with terrific body shots and finally knocked the challenger out in the fourth round. [Heywood] Broun reported, "A gorgeous human will had been beaten down to a point where it could no longer function."

"Your sister next notes that the reporter, Broun, had used the word *fate* four times throughout his piece and then provided several quotes showing how Broun had moved from the objective to the existential:

Paraphrasing now, Broun writes: 'The surprising revelation which came to us on this July afternoon was that a thing may be done well enough to make victory entirely secondary.… All of us who watched Carpentier know now that man cannot beat down Fate, no matter how much his will may flame, but he can rock it back upon its heels when he puts all his heart and the shoulders into a blow.… Eugene O'Neill and all our young writers of tragedy make a great mistake if they think that the poignancy of the fate of man lies in the fact that he is weak, pitiful and helpless. The tragedy of life is not that man loses but that he almost wins.'"

I nodded and said, "You may be on to something there, Jenn. But at this point we just don't know. Everything about Sam is shrouded in mystery, even her disappearance and the fact that she never used her passport again. Perhaps for starters we should revisit the transcript and glean all we can from Sam's own words. Go through it line by line and page by page before we tackle the ton of boxes and set out on the interviews."

"Sounds like a plan. I've got my transcript. Where's your copy, Kyle?"

"In the briefcase under the coffee table there. Should be right on top of the stack of papers."

Jennifer pulled out the case and flipped the locks. "Got it! Here. So how do you want to do this?"

"As before. You read and I'll write on the flip chart. Ready?"

"Ready! Here goes. Page one. Your sister says she has a partner but never mentions the partner by name. If my math is right, your sister was around thirty at the time of the recording and would now be in her early forties. On the disc she says your father is working on adding souls to machines."

"And he still is," I said, "but now as professor emeritus."

"Your sister then says your mother heads up the psychiatric unit at the hospital and has a gallery on the side."

I shook my head and replied, "My mother's retired from medicine now but is still going strong in the African art world."

"Your sister next tells us she has completed eight parts of her 'whale' and has just one part plus a brief epilogue to go. She says she's been living in Saint Petersburg, Russia. Mentions Russian drama and vacationing in the Crimea. We then learn there were thirteen members of the class."

"Of which we have identified five and confirmed interviews with three."

"That's right. Your sister then says she lived in the Babylon district while conducting the class."

"Yes, that's the apartment where my parents found the laptop and some of Sam's effects."

"And when the class gets down to business discussing *Your Winding Daybreak Ways*, they conclude early on your sister intended to write an encyclopedic narrative all along.

During the discussion, they talk about various postmodern characteristics including fragmentation."

"Yes, that's where the first of the marginalia appears—where the Third Tenor says he was having trouble gripping the fragmented narrative, so he rearranged the sections chronologically. He then discovers the rearranged sections move from the external to the internal, from the objective to the subjective, reflecting the sweep of American literature over the past one hundred fifty years. We see that Sam wrote, 'Consider change to chronological narrative' and 'Ted Chandler' in the margin next to the Third Tenor's comments."

"Next, your sister asks the class to determine the total number of narrators for the eight parts of the overall work so far. The class starts at seven and whittles it to six. But your sister respectfully disagrees; and just as she begins revealing the actual number, someone enters the classroom with a message. Your sister leaves without ever explaining the true number of narrators. But sometime later on we see she has written 'ONE!' in the margin next to the Third Alto's estimate of six."

I jumped in again. "Yes, and the emergency must have been pretty serious because it looks like Sam canceled a class or two. When she returns, she says, 'Good to see you again after a week away.' That particular session really got interesting, especially when Sam addresses the questions in the parking lot. Answer number one: she says she plans on using a pseudonym; answer number two, which throws a wrench in your hypothesis, Jenn: Sam says unequivocally *Your Winding Daybreak Ways* is *not* biographical; answer number—"

"I wouldn't be so quick to dismiss my theory just yet," Jennifer said.

"How's that?" I asked. "It's pretty cut and dried, don't you think?"

"But your sister may have been playing with words. Denying the 'biographical' would be a clever way of dodging the revelation that the work is in fact 'autobiographical.' And if that's the case, then my hypothesis is still in play."

"Granted… ," I replied, thinking on it. "Let's park your theory in the 'Unresolved/TBD' issues file for now. So let's see. Where was I?… Oh, answer number three: Sam declares God a co-conspirator and alludes to Brahms's *A German Requiem*; and then finally, answer number four, the pièce de résistance: the way to pick the lock for *Your Winding Daybreak Ways* is in parts six and eight, *McGill* and *Thunderwood*."

Jennifer waved her hand and said, "Two more observations, if you will."

"What's that, Jenn?"

"First, your sister closes each of the sessions with the phrase, 'the gods willing,' and secondly, she has written two additional names in the marginalia—one, Ray Bishov, during the discussion of 'metafiction' where she double underlines the First Bass' assertion, 'You're giving them the map for the road to Hana,' and then a second name, David Jaffe, where the Second Tenor observes that 'African Americans who came to this country as slaves… were an invaluable commodity with very little real worth.'"

"So noted and recorded," I replied. "You think that's a wrap on the transcript, Jenn?"

"As far as I'm concerned, it's a wrap!" she said. "So where to next? The boxes or the interviews?"

"My instinct says the three interviews first. Agree?"

"Agree," she answered, adding, "The more leads we have the merrier."

7

As we neared Old Harbor, the fog began to lift, revealing the Victorian cupolas, gables, and wraparound porches gracing the bluffs overlooking the town docks. Mr. Jaffe's directions instructed us to take a right onto Water Street, a left onto Dodge past the Surf Hotel, and then another right onto Corn Neck Road. He said his cottage was a quarter mile north on the left "nestled up against" Harbor Pond.

When we knocked, a rich tenor rang out, "It's open! Come on in!" We stepped inside to find Mr. Jaffe seated at an easel with his back to us. He was staring out through a wall of glass at a shimmer of sunlight dancing on Parisian blue velvet. As he turned, I said, "Kyle Lynch and Jennifer Townsend, sir. Thank you for agreeing to help us out with our project."

Mr. Jaffe smiled, extended his hand, and replied, "No problem, Kyle. In fact, I've been looking forward to your visit. 'Sam,' as she insisted we call her, had a lasting impact on me, on my approach to painting, and for that matter, my approach to life. Your sister was something special. The atmosphere in the classroom was always electric with every one of us truly engaged in the analyses and discussions of her work. And if it hadn't been for her seminar, these paintings you see hanging on the walls here and on the walls of galleries and museums throughout the US and Europe would have never been painted. She alone helped me find the beauty in the raw canvas."

Jennifer and I turned and surveyed the three walls, each exhibiting six canvases from Mr. Jaffe's private collection. From a distance all the paintings hanging side by side appeared the same—as close to blank canvases as I could imagine. But as Jennifer and I approached the six works to our left on the side wall, we could see the subtle layering as the works "evolved" from left to right. Flying completely blind in my understanding of abstraction, I resorted to the tried-and-true "interesting" but stepped in it when I asked, "Do the six paintings have names?"

Mr. Jaffe smiled and patiently responded, "On no, the six here comprise a single work." To ensure I wouldn't be open to further embarrassment he added, "And the same goes for the oils on the other walls too."

Our resident sculptress weighed in to limit her fiancé's damage. "Metapainting?" she asked.

Mr. Jaffe smiled and looked relieved realizing he wouldn't have to lower the conversational bar too low. "Yes, one of the many takeaways from Sam's class. Each of the three compositions here emphasizes technique as much as evocation of feeling."

Jennifer eased in, asking, "The circularity of being… of our daily lives?"

The artist nodded and quoted Ivory Eboué, "Step beyond the horizon, Jason, and you'll see. The rainbow's a circle. Your descending arc is but the foothills of the next climb."

We all laughed knowingly before I ventured out of my comfort zone again and asked, "Do the *three* compositions here have titles?" I held my breath anxiously awaiting Mr. Jaffe's response.

"Indeed they do, Kyle. The one on the left wall here is *The Burden of Feeling*. The one across the way there is *Sacred Instincts*. And the one on the front wall behind us there is *The Incarnation of What We Can Never Be*."

"The titles, they all sound so familiar," I said.

Mr. Jaffe laughed. "They should, Kyle. They're the titles of Bianca's poems in *McGill*. So you see, there's another example of a takeaway from your sister's class." He paused, looked at his wristwatch, and asked, "What time is your ferry back to Point Judith?"

"Four o'clock," I replied. "We have to drive from there up to Boston tonight. We have another interview scheduled for tomorrow morning across the river in Cambridge."

"You mind my asking with whom you're meeting?"

"With Dr. Ray Bishov. He teaches undergraduate quantum mechanics at MIT."

"Oh yes. I remember Ray well. We all called him 'Square Peg.' He was one of our two 'resident scientists' in the class. We used to hang out together at the Starlight Café drinking espressos and discussing your sister's work. Man, oh man.

I remember he was really into the process, into the art of writing. So please tell 'Square Peg' that 'Brush' says hello."

"By all means. I'm sure he would want to hear from you, know what you've been up to over the past decade since the seminar."

Mr. Jaffe turned and pointed to a rustic ladder leading to the loft. "We'd better get to humping if you've got a four o'clock. I've carved a small study out up there. We can sit down at the desk and review the materials I've pulled together related to the class."

After climbing his primitive "stairway to heaven," we gathered around a manila folder, which he had earlier positioned at the center of his desk. As he opened the file, he offered an apology. "Sad to say, but with all the moving around these are all the notes I've been able to find so far. They're for the first lecture after the Thanksgiving break."

I nearly jumped out of my skin. "Did you say for the *first* lecture *after* the Thanksgiving break?"

"That's right. If my memory serves me, there were at least two if not three lectures all told after Thanksgiving. I was at the first class but missed the last one or two with a fractured hip and femur. Stupid me, my badass motorcycle days landed me in the hospital. But maybe all's not lost. Maybe Square Peg can help you out with the lectures I missed. But anyhow, here's what I've got. That first class after Thanksgiving focused on the motif of appearance and reality. And I must also apologize for the handwriting. It's atrocious."

I asked lightheartedly, "You mind if we come around back and look over your shoulder while you translate your hieroglyphics?"

"No problem," he said. "Come on around back."

Jennifer and I made ourselves as comfortable as we could hunching over the fellow's shoulders. Indeed, the hand-writing was atrocious.

"After someone in the class offered appearance and reality as a motif," Mr. Jaffe began, "Sam asked us for examples supporting the point. I wrote down '*Warfield*—Burns/Parker' and then I have here, 'Thomas fabricates a story about Robert's death to protect the family.'"

"Straightforward so far," I said. "What's next?"

He held the piece of paper up at an angle and said, "Let's see. The note just says, '*Happy Hollow*—Thomas never tells Lil' Jim that he's Lil' Jim's father.' And then it looks like we're on to *Hurricane Creek*. I wrote, 'Lil' Jim appears white,' and then, 'Brutus makes up a story—undertaker and recorder of births, marriages, and deeds,' 'Troy and Lil' Jim hide their homosexuality,' and 'Hurricane Jim reacts to his introduction at the statewide political convention.'"

"Anything for *Hollow Rock*?" I asked.

Mr. Jaffe nodded and replied, "Yes. It looks like I've got a lot of notes for that one. I have here, 'The Christmas presents—the hollow pendant for Margaret and the short cigars for Hurricane Jim'... 'Mrs. Burrows and Hurricane Jim create a win-win façade'... 'The mirrors and the secret passages at The Shanghai'... 'Van and Jacque are not whom they appear to be'... 'Robert Johnson's story'... 'Van becomes Todd's mother/lover/mother in a matter of days'... 'The ministers invest their churches' money in the stock market out of self-interest'... 'Non-believer Todd becomes a minister and sells lots in heaven'..." The artist paused, turned toward us, and mumbled wistfully, "These notes sure bring back the memories. It's almost as if your sister's seminar was yesterday." He shook his head as if trying to clear his mind and said, "Well, that's the last of the 'appearance and reality' motif for *Hollow Rock*. You want to take a break? You've been standing up behind me all this time."

Jennifer and I responded simultaneously, "No, no. Please go on!"

Mr. Jaffe turned the page and said, "Looks like we're now into *McGill*. I wrote, 'the funhouse,' and then jotted a quote in the margin—'Beyond the vestibule we entered the labyrinthine Maze of Mirrors, which distorted our bodies into countless shapes.' Next to that I wrote, '*The Golden Bowl*' and another quote: 'The smiling, scheming couple quietly announced, "check!" But Maggie counterattacked; and with growing insight of the adulterous affair, she methodically set about clearing the board and stealthily separating the furtive pair for good.' Then I've got here 'research exercise—don't believe everything you read in the newspapers' and 'Talley and Sanders hide their homosexuality.' And finally I wrote, 'Bianca's note to Andrew in Portuguese.' He paused again, turned in his chair, and asked, "Is all this making sense to you? I mean, some of it does for me but other parts I've written here I've just simply forgotten."

I patted Mr. Jaffe on the shoulder and reassured him, "No worries, sir. Believe me, Jenn and I are very familiar with the material. You're certainly not wasting your or our time. This is a great help. So, please, please go on."

Encouraged by our positive feedback, Mr. Jaffe lengthened his spine and returned to his notes. "Well, it looks like we've moved on to *Cabedelo*. It says here the professor reveals all in a tape recording—Catherine and he were lovers and parents to Samuel. Bianca and he were lovers and the parents of Danielle. Which means Samuel and his lover, Danielle, are stepbrother and sister!" Mr. Jaffe turned the page, paused, and then turned around to face us again. All the while he kept tapping his index finger on the latest page. He finally said, "So that brings us to the last few minutes of that post-Thanksgiving lecture. The few minutes that changed my life forever."

"The section? The subject?" Jennifer asked earnestly.

"The eighth section, *Thunderwood*. I remember this as if it were yesterday. It was during the discussion of Velázquez's painting, *The Maids of Honor*. After one of us in the class offered Bones's analysis of the painting as an example of the 'appearance and reality' motif, Sam appeared to become energized and uncharacteristically took command of the discussion and literally read the passage word for word. I was so moved by her words and actions that after class I went back to my apartment and copied the two relevant paragraphs from my draft manuscript into my notebook here." Mr. Jaffe turned back around and began reading just as Sam had done some ten years before:

On the surface the painting, *Las Meninas*, or *The Maids of Honor*, appears to be a straightforward rendering of some of the key figures in King Philip IV's court. You have the young princess, Margaret Theresa, surrounded by her entourage, including her bodyguard, her chaperone, two handmaidens, two dwarfs, and a dog. The artist includes himself in the picture. He's standing at a large canvas immediately *behind* and to the right of the princess and her entourage, staring out beyond the frame toward the viewer and painting a composition positioned well outside the pictorial space.

But the plot thickens. First, what's the subject of the work Velázquez depicts himself painting? And second, if this is a "commissioned portrait of the royal family," where are King Philip IV and his queen, Mariana? The answers to both questions are captured in a mirror hanging on the far wall behind the princess, her entourage, and the painter. The mirror reflects the torsos and heads of the king and queen. But is the image a likeness of them standing outside the pictorial space alongside the viewer or is it a reflection of the canvas Velázquez is currently painting?

What's the reality here?

After reading the passage, Mr. Jaffe turned back around to face us. "And I'll never forget," he said, "when your sister finished the paragraphs, she stared out the window and whispered the last lines of the first paragraph again: 'He's standing at a large canvas immediately behind and to the right of the princess and her entourage, staring out beyond the frame toward the viewer.' Sam then repeated the phrase, 'toward the viewer,' twice. And that was the very instant metapainting became a reality for me. Paintings about the process of painting."

All Jenn and I could do to respond to his reverie was nod our heads and fall back on another tried-and-true phrase: "Fascinating, Mr. Jaffe. Fascinating."

When the spell broke, the artist smiled, shrugged his shoulders, and said, "Well, that's it. Sorry, but that's all I've got for you."

I patted him on the shoulder again and reassured him, "Believe me, sir, you've helped us more than you'll ever know."

Jennifer nodded and added, "That's for sure, Mr. Jaffe. Kyle and I will never forget our trip out here to see you on this glorious October day."

8

IT WAS AS IF the gods had stepped in now to help advance the story. Where David Jaffe had found extensive notes on Sam's first lecture after Thanksgiving, Dr. Bishov at MIT had located only mere fragments, but they fortuitously pertained to that critical second session, which Mr. Jaffe had missed because of his accident and subsequent hospitalization.

As we knocked on the office door, a thin man with a full beard and shock of wiry gray hair rushed up behind us with key in hand and said, "I'm so sorry! I lost track of time. Several of my students and I got wrapped around Schrödinger's equation. Here, let me get the door for you." After briefly fumbling with the lock, he managed to open the door and motioned for us to enter. As he hung his blazer on an antique coat stand at the back of the room, he reeled off several commands one after another: "Make yourselves at home. Forgive the mess. Just slide the books and papers beneath the chairs there and take a seat."

When I sensed an opening, I jumped in. "By the way, Dr. Bishov, before I forget it, the 'Brush' said to tell 'Square Peg' hello."

As the professor settled into his chair behind the desk, he paused and stared at me as if I had just landed here from another planet. He said, "I beg your pardon?"

I repeated the message.

The professor shook his head and replied, "I'm sorry. Who again?"

I responded embarrassedly, "The Brush. David Jaffe. The painter. Block Island. A member of my sister's class with you."

Dr. Bishov began nodding and replied haltingly, "Oh yes, yes. Old Dave Jaffe." But the "what-the-fuck" glance he was giving me told me everything; the professor didn't have a clue who this David "the Brush" Jaffe was or who he had ever been.

Jennifer stepped in to save the day. "So we understand, sir, you have some notes from Samantha Lynch's seminar on *Your Winding Daybreak Ways*."

"Ah, yes, that's right. Just a few, from one of the last lectures." The professor leaned over and pulled a file from his briefcase. He dropped the folder on the desk and opened it, revealing what looked to be no more than two to three pages of printer paper with some tiny scribbling running up the page at a decided angle. He scanned the opening lines with his index finger and then read from the first page. "It says here, 'Soldiering on.' And then it looks like I've listed a number of references."

"For example, sir?"

"It says, '*Warfield*—Beth leaves. Thomas senses he can't go on. Despair keeps pounding him to his knees but remembers Master Hudson will return within the month. Must keep moving until then. Thomas believes no one understands how much pain he feels or realizes how hard it will be for him to get back into the routine of things.'" Dr. Bishov paused, looked up, and said, "I then have a direct quote here."

"Please go on, sir," Jennifer said.

"Well, the quote says, 'And it was while lying in bed on the bleakest of those nights, I learned that the dark could help illuminate the light.'"

Jennifer smiled and said, "It's one of my favorite passages, Dr. Bishov." After a brief reflective pause, she encouraged the professor to continue deciphering his notes.

He scanned the rest of the first page and said, "Well, it looks like we're now in *Happy Hollow*. I've written, 'Aaron's essay on how authors view physical phenomena in moral and/or psychological terms—despite death, alienation, and bleakness all around them, most Greeks, Romans, Byzantines, Italians, and English remained optimistic their nightmares would end. Aaron argues that under such daunting pressure this hopeful optimism was transformed into a calm courage—the inexplicable, death-defying courage to act on behalf of others. So these brave souls continued on. They demonstrated an unspeakable love for family, friends, and strangers.'"

Dr. Bishov paused again to read the next entries and then paraphrased, "I noted here Thomas displays that same death-defying courage during the yellow fever epidemics in Memphis. Even though he's a doctor, he goes outside to vomit after discovering a pile of bones lying in a puddle of slime. And then I have here 'Reverend Woodburn's Thanksgiving sermon—he praises the thousands of strangers who came to Memphis with the courage to carry on despite the risks to their own lives. The reverend declares heroism ruled the day and describes these priests, nuns, doctors, and nurses as a noble army of martyrs who heard the Lord's promise, He that hateth his life in this world shall keep it unto life eternal.'"

"That's great, Dr. Bishov. What's next?" I asked eagerly.

The professor read a few more lines. "Looks like another Reverend Woodburn exhortation. A special Christmas message a month following his laudatory Thanksgiving Day sermon. I wrote here, 'The reverend bases his talk on an unusual scripture for the holidays—sixth chapter of Saint Paul's letter to the Hebrews. But in the context of the recent epidemic, the reverend's choice of text makes a lot of sense. Saint Paul urges the Hebrews to lay hold upon the hope set before us, which hope we have as an anchor of the soul.' I then wrote down a direct quote from Thomas, who senses he and the reverend are on the same page. Would you like me to read it?"

"Oh yes, please, sir." Jenn and I both nodded encouragingly.

Dr. Bishov read:

> So I'm not alone. I've been preaching that gospel
> in my office since the beginning of November.
> Things have changed, but in some ways they've
> stayed the same—I no longer make the daily
> rounds trying desperately to treat the yellow jack.
> No. I spend most of my time now in the office

treating broken hearts. Just as daunting a task
as the yellow jack, just as lethal, and all I had to
offer them was hope.

"Do you have any idea why you chose to copy this particular quote into your notes?" I asked.

Dr. Bishov stroked his beard for a few seconds and then answered, "I suspect it was because your sister had quoted the passage herself during the lecture. I now recall that toward the end of the series of classes, she became much more engaged in the discussions—you know, offering insights and reading a number of paragraphs from her work."

The professor then turned the page and said, "Looks like I only have a few lines left here. I wrote, '*Hollow Rock*—Pastor Dives prays the Lord will grant the mourners the courage to face the days to come. *Cabedelo*—Beckett: I cannot go on. I must go on. Try again. Fail again. Fail better. *Thunderwood*—Ishiguro: There is nothing for it but to try and see our missions through to the end, as best we can. Jason says the Outcasts found the gritty determination to exist.' And finally I have here Peter Abelard's medieval lyric: 'In heaven there won't be a separation between wish and fulfillment. All prayers will be answered. But in the meantime we just have to soldier on.'" Dr. Bishov looked up from the page and said, "Well, I hope these few scraps will be helpful in your endeavor."

I smiled and replied, "No worries, sir. There's more than enough here to feed the multitudes."

The professor nodded and smiled appreciatively. He then stood up, extended his hand, and added, "And when you see Mr. Jaffe again, Mr. Lynch, tell him I said hello."

I looked over at Jennifer and smiled. Looking back at Dr. Bishov I said, "With pleasure, sir. I'm sure he'll be happy to hear from you."

Since our meeting with Ted Chandler was scheduled for the following morning and it was peak foliage season in New England besides, Jennifer and I drove the scenic route across the commonwealth to Williamstown where Professor Chandler taught. His email instructed us to drive from our bed-and-breakfast over to the Art Institute on South Street, park the car, and take the hiking trail up to the Stone Hill Center where we could attend an all-important retrospective of David Smith's painted *Circle* series, commune with nature on the wooded paths, and discuss his "very limited recollections" of my sister's seminar. He added a cautionary postscript to his email, warning us he didn't have a single note from any of the lectures.

So after touring the Smith sculpture exhibition the following morning, Dr. Chandler guided us out onto one of his favorite walking paths and opened a monologue in medias res. "The last class, you see, was truncated. It was nowhere near the usual hour and fifteen minutes to an hour and a half. It lasted no more than thirty minutes, and what was unusual was your sister did all the talking. She seemed to be in a hurry, trying to squeeze in as much thought as she could before time ran out." The professor paused and shook his head. "I'll never forget that last lecture. It was all about rainbows."

After what happened next you could have knocked Jennifer and me over with a feather. Contrary to our expectations of limited recollections and no notes, the professor began quoting verbatim what Sam had had to say about rainbows that day in class. He even included a direct quote from *Happy Hollow*:

> I stroked the side of Hannah's face gently with the back of my hand and said lightheartedly, "Do I see a little rainbow there?"
>
> "Rainbow?" she murmured.
>
> "Your smile. That's what Mama used to say to us children when she'd tease us to make us laugh when we'd be crying about something. As we got older, she added another thought about the rainbow. She'd say, 'The rainbow takes you to the joy on the far side of sadness.' None of us really understood the meaning until we got a lot older and everyone started dying around us during the war. Finding a way to share a laugh or a smile helped us survive the horrors we saw every day.'

She gazed into my eyes and repeated, "The far side of sadness."

"When your sister finished reading that passage, she closed her notebook, stared out the window for a good half minute or more and then moved to the door. She turned, whispered something to the effect, 'To be continued' or 'To be done,' and then disappeared into the hallway. And that's the last any of us ever saw of her. Strange to vanish like that." Professor Chandler paused again and smiled. "But there was one good thing to come out of all this," he said.

"What's that?" I asked.

"Your sister had somehow prearranged it with the administrative staff to ensure we all got the A's she had promised us at the beginning of the class."

Jennifer and I looked at each other and smiled.

9

Jennifer looked up from the Sunday *New York Times* and said, "I hate to be a pain in the ass, but the more we review the texts, transcript, and interviews, the more convinced I am *Your Winding Daybreak Ways* reflects your sister's feelings in real time. It's the pendulum imagery and the wide swings in narrative from crushing despair to guarded hope and then back again to the lowest depths of hell. Track the major sections chronologically. It's as if everything was going extremely well for your sister, next the loomings, then the world seems to come crashing down around her, and finally, there's this sense of acceptance with a grim resolve to carry on.

"But there's much more than the pendulum imagery and the narrative arc that's eating at me. My God, the motifs, Kyle! Look at the motifs. 'Loss' from *Warfield* to *Thunderwood*. 'The Existential Why?' from beginning to end. 'False Appearances and Reality' from first part to last. The multiple meanings of 'Rainbows' and then finally, an imperative to 'Soldier On' despite the losses and the suffering."

"So you still think we should pursue Sam's biography?"

"Yes. I hate to keep harping on it, but somehow, someway we should try finding out what happened to your sister before, during, and after the seminar. Whatever it was that was going on appears to have stimulated her to start writing fiction and continue on for at least another five years. It surely won't cost you anything but a little time. And who knows? If you can establish a strong connection between her life and work, it will certainly add insight and richness to your analyses. So what have you really got to lose? And besides, we might even get lucky for a change."

"Okay, Jenn, I'll grant you a major discovery like that would strengthen the scholarship. But honestly, it still seems like a long shot. I mean a real Hail Mary. Where would we begin? Try finding more participants and then conducting additional interviews with the hopes of striking pay dirt?"

"Well, before you decide one way or the other, let me lay one last card on the table."

"What's that?" I asked.

"Remember when one of the students asked your sister how to 'pick the lock' for *Your Winding Daybreak Ways*?"

"Sure. Go on."

"Remember how she answered?"

"Yes. Sam said, '*McGill* and *Thunderwood*.'"

"That's right. And while I'm sure part of the answer lies in the chess shorthand at the beginning of each chapter of *McGill*, I'm equally sure another part of the answer lies in Andrew's description of a student's term paper." Jennifer picked up her copy of *McGill*, which had been lying open on the kitchen table, and began reading:

> Instead, Donna chose a passage from Fiedler's initial paragraph as the basis for her final work:

> "Most of my best literary friends, at any rate, considered it strategically advisable to speak of novels and poems purely (the adverb is theirs) in terms of diction, structure, and point of view—remaining safely inside the realm of the format."

> Donna opened with a broadside against the New Criticism movement established at Vanderbilt in the early 1920s and espoused by such respected scholars, poets, and writers as Warren, Brooks, Ransom, Tate, Riding, and Moore. She disagreed with their notion that each literary work should stand on its own and be analyzed in a vacuum, with no regard either for its cultural and historical milieu or the author's likely intentions. Donna believed rejecting these highly effective interpretive tools severely limited the reader's ability to fully appreciate the power, scope, and meaning of the overall work.

Jennifer laid the manuscript back down on the table, smiled, and said confidently, "I don't know how it strikes you, but to me the passage screams, 'Biography! Biography!'"

I laughed and responded, "Okay, okay. We'll add Sam's biography to our plates. But first things first. Our next task is to start cataloging all the material archived in that room full of boxes back there."

Jennifer laughed, extended her hand playfully, and said, "Let's shake on it. Agreed?"

10

JENNIFER'S SCREAM TOLD ME she might have hit the mother lode. I raced to the back room and found her sitting on the floor riffling through the contents of one of the boxes. I asked excitedly, "What you got there, Jenn?"

She gave me her signature cat-ate-the-canary smile and replied, "We now have another marked-up copy of the manuscript, some books, and a bookmark."

"And that deserves a banshee shriek?"

She nodded and answered confidently, "It sure does. I think we really have something this time."

"But you said you've found more books. My God, Jenn, you know we already have most if not all of Sam's personal library packed away in here."

Jennifer shook her head and smiled.

"And you say you found another iteration of *Your Winding Daybreak Ways*. Geez. We must have close to a dozen versions by now."

She shook her head again and smiled.

"Which leaves me hanging my hat on an irrelevant bookmark. So tell me, Jenn, seriously, what's all the excitement about?"

"First, the edits to the manuscript are not in Sam's hand. You can see for yourself. You said your sister is left-handed and her letters slant to the left. The script here leans to the right, most likely signifying a right-handed individual making the edits. Next, the books are inscribed 'To my dearest Marta.' And finally, the pièce de résistance."

"What's that?" I asked. My excitement was bubbling over.

"Your 'irrelevant' bookmark," she teased.

"Okay, so let's back up and go through these one at a time. First of all, did you find anything else in the manuscript that could help advance the cause?"

"Hey, I'm quick, but not that quick! You have to remember I just got my hands on these things less than fifteen minutes ago."

"Well then, are there any clues lurking in the books? I mean, who is this Marta? Any ideas?"

This time Jennifer nodded and said, "I might be able to help you out with that one."

"Okay, so help me out. Who is Marta?"

Jennifer handed me a thin brochure. "That's the bookmark I found folded lengthwise in Marta's copy of *Harmonium: Poems by Wallace Stevens.* And you know which poem Marta had bookmarked and underlined extensively?"

I shook my head.

"'Sunday Morning.' Remember? *Hollow Rock*. It was one of Van's favorite poems."

"And one of mine as well," I said. Then I whispered the last four lines:

> And, in the isolation of the sky,
> At evening, casual flocks of pigeons make
> Ambiguous undulations as they sink,
> Downward to darkness, on extended wings.

"Kyle, do you remember the dialogue between Todd and Van about those last few lines?"

I nodded as she began quoting their bittersweet exchange:

> After a long, reflective silence, I whispered,
> "What do you make of these last lines, Van?"

> She gazed into my eyes and replied wistfully, "I
> hear acceptance. That her dream will never be
> fulfilled as imagined."

"So you see, Kyle, we have here another good example of the 'soldiering on' theme."

I nodded, paused briefly, and then read aloud the front cover of the brochure: "Third Annual International Young Writers' Colloquium. Georgetown University. Washington, DC."

"And check the date!" Jennifer said. "The conference was some seventeen years ago!"

I smiled. "But the bookmark's the pièce de résistance? How so?"

"Open it. Read the names of the attendees. Under 'Poetry' you'll find your sister and then under 'Theater' you'll see 'Marta Eshchenko.'"

I jumped in, speculating, "Perhaps they met there at the conference. Formed a friendship—or even more."

"Yes, and maybe there's a way to find out," Jennifer said.

"I'm all ears."

"Why not contact the conference coordinator listed there? I mean, if Professor Brody is still around Georgetown teaching, maybe he could provide a lead or two. And if he says he might have something for us, why not hop the high-speed and interview him face-to-face in DC? And then, you know, make a weekend of it. I haven't been to Washington since I was a little girl."

It was only two days later that Jennifer and I were climbing the front steps of a luxury condo just off the Georgetown campus and ringing the bell. A short, slightly overweight, balding Professor Brody answered the door and said drolly, "Please, come on in. It's modest, but we call it home." He then motioned for us to follow him up the staircase to his study, which was lined with books from floor to ceiling on three walls. "Please, take a seat there," he said. "Would you like something to drink before we get down to business?"

Jennifer and I shook our heads and answered in unison, "No, thanks."

"You sure? It's god-awful hot here this time of year."

We answered again in unison, "We're sure."

"Well, let me grab my file off the desk over there, and I'll be right back."

When he returned, the professor settled into an over-stuffed Empire chair, scanned his notes, and opened the conversation: "As we discussed on the telephone, Kyle, I met your sister and Marta for the first time at that young writers forum some seventeen years ago. At that point Samantha had published brief lyrics in respected literary journals and Marta had written and directed her first of many experimental plays at the renowned Liteiny Theater in Saint Petersburg, Russia." He paused to relight his stubborn pipe and continued. "Well, I guess it's okay to admit it now, but those two were my favorites of all the participants. They showed so much promise; and forgive me, Jennifer, their looks didn't hurt them one bit either. So when the conference ended, Marta and I exchanged letters occasionally for some two or three years before she stopped responding to my mail. But with your sister, Samantha, it was totally different. We corresponded for a good seven or so years after the conference ended. I got letters from everywhere. First from Maui, then New York, Lisbon, Copenhagen. And after that, Saint Petersburg, where Samantha always added a postscript, 'Marta says to tell you hello.'"

"When was the last time you heard from Samantha?" Jennifer asked.

Professor Brody stroked his graying beard and replied, "Some ten or so years ago. She wrote that she was back in the States for a while conducting a seminar at Pantheon University. It was postmarked Warfield, Tennessee."

"Did Samantha say anything else?" I probed. "I mean, like her plans for the future?"

"No. Nothing like that."

"You mind sharing what else she had to say in that last correspondence?"

"No, not at all. I suspect her real reason for writing was to alert me to a talented graduate student attending her seminar."

After quickly glancing over at me, Jennifer asked eagerly, "Do you recall the student's name or anything about them?"

Professor Brody laughed and replied, "I sure do. He just earned tenure here at Georgetown this past year."

I couldn't believe what I was hearing. "You say this fellow attended Samantha's workshop at Pantheon some ten years ago and now he teaches here?"

"That's right."

"Ah, is there any way we can talk to him?" I asked.

"I'm sure that can be arranged, but you'll have to stay the weekend. Professor Lyons is supposed to be back on campus Monday morning for a departmental meeting, and I'm sure he would enjoy speaking with you."

Jennifer responded, "As a matter of fact, I twisted Kyle's arm into staying the weekend and doing some sightseeing. We were going to make our hotel reservations when we finished speaking with you."

"Nonsense," Professor Brody replied as he began waving his arms about. "We have plenty of space to accommodate you here at the Brody Resort!"

"We couldn't impose on you like that," Jennifer demurred.

"Oh, yes, you could, and yes, you should. I insist. Besides, the resort offers complimentary guided tours to the most popular landmarks in and around DC. So how could you resist the offer? What do you say?"

I laughed. "Okay, if you insist. So what time is checkout on Monday?"

He puffed on his pipe, then smiled and said, "One hour before your scheduled meeting with Professor Lyons."

So after a whirlwind tour of the best restaurants and tourist sites DC had to offer, Professor Brody escorted us over to the Georgetown English department late Monday morning and introduced us to his colleague, Dr. Thomas Lyons. The professor did the honors. "Tom, I would like to introduce you to Ms. Lynch's brother, Kyle, and his fiancée, Jennifer Townsend."

The handsome, dark-eyed scholar extended his hand and said, "Tom Lyons. Nice to meet the two of you."

I shook his hand and said, "It's nice to meet you too, sir. And thank you for agreeing to spend a few minutes with Jennifer and me discussing that long-ago seminar in the middle of nowhere."

"No problem at all. I—"

"I'm sorry folks," Dr. Brody said, breaking in. "I'd like to stay, but I have another meeting to prepare for tomorrow afternoon."

I extended my hand to Dr. Brody and said, "Thanks again for everything, sir—the use of your house over the weekend, the fine tours, and the lead, which hooked us up with Professor Lyons here."

"No problem, Kyle. And good luck to the two of you with your research. I'm looking forward to reading the work Samantha produced following our writers forum here."

As Professor Brody disappeared into the hallway, Dr. Lyons motioned for us to take a seat near his ornately carved mahogany desk. He opened the conversation with an apology: "Because of the short notice, I didn't have the time to pull anything together for you. I know I still have my copies of the manuscripts and some notes packed away somewhere at the house in the archives. I'll scan and email anything relevant once I can lay my hands on it." He then pointed to his temple with his forefinger and continued, "But for today I guess we'll just have to rely on what I've got stored up here in the memory bank."

"No problem, sir," I said. "But since we have a recording of the lectures before Thanksgiving, why don't you focus on any recollections you have of the sessions after the holiday."

"Well, let's see. If my memory serves me right, most of the lectures following Thanksgiving were similar in nature to the ones you already have recorded. They were over an hour long, with Ms. Lynch asking the questions while providing little feedback."

Jennifer jumped in. "Excuse me, sir, did you say *most* of the lectures?"

The professor nodded and replied, "Yes, that's right, because I distinctly remember our last meeting was very short and Ms. Lynch did all the talking." He paused and smiled before adding, "I remember now. The lecture was all about rainbows. Like she was dreaming of being someplace else— Hawaii, Tahiti, or some other Pacific paradise."

"Yes, that's right," Jennifer said. "We heard something similar to that during another of our participant interviews." She glanced down at her notes and asked, "Do you remember anything else unusual about any of the other post-Thanksgiving lectures?"

"Hmm, let's see. Well, this didn't have anything to do with the content or format of the lecture but with where we held the meeting. It was not at the usual place, I mean. It wasn't on campus in the tenth-floor conference room."

"So where did she hold that particular session?" I asked eagerly.

"It was at your sister's rental home over in the Babylon district."

"Do you remember much about the meeting?" Jennifer asked.

"Funny. I mean the things you remember after all these years. I don't recall much about the lecture. That's where my notes will come in handy. But I remember brief flashes, vignettes: a digital photo frame, a brochure, a bedroom."

I interrupted impatiently, "A digital photo frame? Of what? Of whom?"

"A series of photographs. The one I remember was of your sister and another young woman, sitting at the rim of a crater with a bank of white-gray clouds hovering behind them. They were wearing ball caps with sweaters wrapped loosely around their shoulders, gazing lovingly into each other's eyes. Smiling. Locked in a warm embrace."

Jenn and I looked at each other excitedly. Everything was beginning to fall into place. I pressed Dr. Lyons. "And the brochure?"

"An up-to-the-minute pamphlet, 'Maui Forever.' It was sitting on a drum table next to the digital frame. I perused it while we were waiting for Ms. Lynch to reappear. I remember it clearly because the pictures and the brochure were out of sync."

"What do you mean 'out of sync'?" Jennifer asked.

"I don't know. It just seemed odd. The pictures of them in paradise *predated* the brochure. Not vice versa. Ms. Lynch—and I guess the partner whom she told us about in class—looked different in the pictures than they did when we visited the house."

"How's that?" I probed.

"Your sister appeared a few years younger in the photographs, and her partner... well... " He paused and shook his head.

"Please go on," I urged.

"So let me explain. I asked to use the bathroom; and as I walked down the hallway, I looked to my left into a bedroom where the woman in the photographs was propped up on pillows sleeping. She looked tired. Pale. Older than her age."

Jennifer interrupted, playing devil's advocate. "Maybe she was just suffering the flu or something like that. You know, any of us can look tired, old, and pale when we're sick."

The professor shook his head. "No, no. It didn't appear temporary like that."

"How do you know for sure?" I asked.

"A wheelchair was positioned beside the bed. Sad to say, whatever it was appeared to be both serious and chronic."

"Anything else you remember about your visit?"

He stroked his chin pensively and said, "No, I can't think of anything else special." Professor Lyons then stood up and extended his hand. "Well, I hope this has been helpful."

"You can't imagine, sir," I replied. "Thank you for your time."

He smiled appreciatively and said, "And remember now I'll email you the other material as soon as I find it. I have a pretty good idea where it's hiding."

Jennifer extended her hand and said, "We look forward to reviewing it, sir. Thanks again."

"Have a safe trip back home to Tennessee," he said as he escorted us over to the door.

"The gods willing," I replied. "The gods willing."

11

As SHE FOLDED THE map she had been examining and filed it away in one of the miscellaneous folders, Jennifer said, "Things are really coming into focus now. Where do you want to go from here?"

"Why don't we take a breather and summarize what we know before digging into more of the boxes? How about the same modus operandi as before? You give me your significant findings to date, and I'll post them on the flip chart. What do you say?"

"Sounds like a plan. Well, first of all, a global observation. I'm convinced now more than ever your sister's writing reflects her feelings in real time. I mean, based on everything we've learned from the interviews, *Your Winding Daybreak Ways* appears to correlate nicely with your sister's life. Agreed?"

I smiled and replied, "Agnostic but leaning your way. Granted, your theory has become more plausible, but I'm still not entirely on board yet. So why don't you make a rigorous case from axiom to proof?" I uncapped the marker with a dramatic flair and said, "Convince me! I'm ready to copy."

"Okay. Here goes then." Jennifer took a deep breath and presented her findings to date: "When a bright, sensitive young woman, Samantha, reaches escape velocity, she moves to Nashville and attends Vanderbilt University following in the footsteps of leading twentieth-century American poets. Her dream has always been to become a poet, that is, until fate steps in and changes her life and career forever.

"She attends a young writers' conference at Georgetown University and falls deeply in love with her soul mate, Marta Eshchenko, a beautiful young Russian playwright. On a whim they fly to Hawaii, explore the islands, and choose a favorite, Maui. Photographs of the two lovers on the crater's rim fail to fully capture the depth of feeling they share for one another. They are living the dream. There is no question now the thumb is on the scale in their favor. How could life become any sweeter?

"The poet and the dramatist then fly to New York where the American lyricist is living at the time. They spend a few bittersweet days together before the Russian boards her outbound flight to Saint Petersburg. The inside addresses of the poet's letters now begin to chart an ever-tightening orbit as she is inexorably drawn to the love of a lifetime—first, letters from New York. Next from Lisbon. Then from Cologne and Copenhagen. And finally, correspondence back to the States from her lover's Saint Petersburg address. The balance beam continues to move in their favor."

"But no," I eased in, "the thumb on the scale can't allow too much pleasure or happiness here. Pain is its realm; suffering its purview. So, the thumb now begins sliding away from the star-crossed pair. The gods have declared war on the lovers, and the omnipotent know where to find the loose threads that unravel the soul. The lovers are now pulled down and swallowed by chasms. Marta suffers some catastrophic accident or illness. Fear flows like blood inside their bodies. Sam and Marta hold each other throughout a sleepless night, as if vainly trying to prevent something precious from slipping away. But no one up there is listening. The mood darkens. The lovers have somehow arced from youthful innocence to existential nothingness."

Jennifer picked up the narrative. "So questions abound now. The supplicants are reduced to thrusting their arms into the air and assertively asking, 'Why?' It doesn't make any sense to them, a death sentence so soon after birth. Why the compression? Why the non sequitur? Why make them the butt of a cosmic joke? Samantha sits braced against the wide, gray trunk of a linden tree holding Marta in her arms, stroking her hair, and whispering, 'Why, Jesus? Why?' Why is everything to be denied? / That could make life a little bright. Why is it that you allow us to *almost* win?"

When Jennifer paused to take a sip of her tea, I jumped in again. "The pendulum now begins to swing. Sam inexplicably revels one day in frenetic, euphoric highs and the next suffers debilitating, unspeakable lows. She realizes now unpredictability is the insidious constant that the devious geniuses have embedded in the organic formulae. She knows now that she can't beat down Fate, no matter how hard she tries, but she can rock it back on its heels when she puts her soul into a strong counterpunch."

And then it was Jennifer's turn to weigh in again. "While lying in bed on the bleakest of nights, Samantha discovers that perhaps the dark could help illuminate the light. Under such daunting pressure her hopeful optimism is now transformed into a calm courage to act on the behalf of Marta and others who might someday read her works. Samantha will no longer make the daily rounds but spend her time now writing, treating broken hearts with all she has to offer—an inextinguishable, death-defying hope that there will no longer be a separation between wish and fulfillment. Samantha has found a gritty determination to exist, to see her mission through to the end, to soldier on, choosing the slow-flaming breadth and depth of fiction to the brief, searing intensity of poetry. And thus *Your Winding Daybreak Ways* is born."

I moved toward the couch, gazed into Jennifer's eyes, and asked, "If, as we imagine, Sam's encyclopedic narrative closely tracks her life, what happens next? At this point both the narrative and her life remain open-ended."

Jennifer smiled and responded provocatively, "That's up to you, Kyle. What happens next is now up to you."

"What do you mean?"

"My gut's telling me your sister wants you to finish her story."

"Complete the research and editing? For my thesis?"

"No. I believe she's left you several strong clues signaling you should finish writing *Your Winding Daybreak Ways*."

"Complete Sam's work?"

"That's right. She left everything behind. If she intended on finishing the narrative, she would have taken all the material with her."

I pushed back mildly: "Maybe Sam planned on coming back and finishing it later."

"That's a stretch, in my opinion. If she had planned on coming back, she would have left specific instructions on how to handle the manuscripts, notes, and the like. She's been gone for years now, Kyle. And besides, we have the hints in the manuscript and the interviews. Take, for example, the discussion of Velázquez's masterpiece in *Thunderwood*, which, by the way, your sister says is vital to 'picking the overall lock.' Mr. Jaffe said your sister read a key passage aloud in class: 'The artist includes himself in the picture. He's standing at a large canvas immediately behind and to the right of the princess and her entourage, staring out beyond the frame toward the viewer and painting a composition positioned well outside the pictorial space.' Mr. Jaffe added that Samantha whispered these lines again and then repeated the phrase, 'toward the viewer,' twice. The artist is looking out at *you* while working on an *unfinished* masterpiece."

I shook my head. "I was on board with you until the last part, Jenn. I think that's where your argument breaks down. In reality, Velázquez did finish his painting. There was nothing left for anyone else to do."

Jennifer smiled and said, "That's what Velázquez assumed too when he *thought* he had completed the work in 1656. But after Velázquez's death, King Philip decreed the red cross of the Order of Santiago be added to Velázquez's chest in the painting. The king wanted to honor his dear friend. He wanted the added cross to reflect the artist's entrance into the Spanish knighthood a good three years *after* Velázquez had ostensibly finished *The Maids of Honor*." She paused to assess my reaction. "That look of yours tells me you still need some convincing, right?"

I nodded and she continued her argument.

"Okay then, let's take another example from *Thunderwood*. Remember the conversation between Jason and Ivory about Bach's purported last work, *Die Kunst der Fuge*?"

"Yes... and I think I know where you're going with this. But go on."

Jennifer shuffled through a pile of manuscripts, found *Thunderwood*, and then read the relevant passage aloud, beginning with Jason correctly playing "name that tune":

> "Okay, okay. It's old Bach's last work, *Die Kunst der Fuge*. Like Mahler's *Tenth*. Left unfinished at death. Ah, what did Bach's son write on the last page of the manuscript?"

> "C.P.E. wrote, 'At the point where the composer introduces the name *BACH*'—you know, B♭-A-C-B♮—'in the countersubject to this fugue, the composer died.' But I'm not buying it, Jason.... The last pages are in Bach's hand,

and they are very clean. They had to have been written at some time before his sight failed and his handwriting became practically illegible."

"But why would he leave his work unfinished like that? Doesn't make any sense."

"Of course it does. He left it for us…. For us to continue…. I'm convinced he left it for us to pick up his recursions and continue on."

"Got to hand it to you, Ivory, that's a fascinating idea. Trusting us mortals to carry on with his argument."

This time Jennifer didn't stop to judge my reaction. She was on a mission to convince me I had a sacred responsibility—an obligation—not only to my sister but to her potential readers as well. She raced on to a third and final point. "And we have evidence beyond Samantha's work. I mean in the interviews as well. Remember? Professor Chandler described that last class, the one where your sister talked about rainbows, foothills, and next climbs. The professor said when she finished reading the last lines from *Thunderwood*, she closed her notebook, stared out the window briefly, and then moved to the door. He said Samantha turned, whispered something to the effect, 'To be continued' or 'To be done,' and then disappeared into the hallway." Jennifer paused now, gazed into my eyes, and asked, "Could it be any clearer, Kyle? Could it be any clearer what your sister really wants you to do?"

I smiled with admiration, raised my hands, and responded, "*No mas*, Jenn! *No mas*!"

12

"THE NEXT QUESTION THEN IS where do we get the answers? How can we ever finish Sam's leviathan when two of the major players disappear without a trace after the 'rainbow' seminar?"

"Easy," Jennifer said with a smile. "We just have to discover where your sister and Marta went and find out what happened to them after that. The rest of the narrative will practically write itself. You'll see."

I shook my head. "I wish I shared your optimism, Jenn. But having said that, let's get started on this fool's errand. So tell me, where do you think we should begin?"

"If, as we believe, your sister wanted you to finish *Your Winding Daybreak Ways*, she would have naturally provided signposts to her and Marta's whereabouts. And where might she stow these clues? Most likely in her notes, in the transcript, the manuscript, and if you want to go out on the speculative limb a bit, you would include our face-to-face interviews, which she would have surely envisioned." Jennifer paused and then asked, "So taking all these primary sources into consideration, Kyle, where do you think your sister and

Marta went after leaving McGill? The authorities told your parents Samantha never used her passport again after traveling to Pantheon, so they have to be somewhere in the States."

"Well, based on some of Sam's last work, I would have to say they went back to Washington."

"Why's that?" Jennifer asked.

"In *Thunderwood* Zulu has all the Outcasts speaking Russian. She studies theater in Saint Petersburg and winds up working for a theater in DC, which, by the way, is where three of the four Outcasts end up after being graduated from Pantheon."

Jennifer nodded slowly and gave me her polite "I'm-not-buying-it" response, "Interesting."

"So what's your take on their whereabouts, Jenn?"

"I'm leaning toward Maui."

I challenged her lightheartedly, "Okay then. Axiom to proof."

"First, the photographs of the lovers on the rim of the crater. Next, the up-to-date pamphlet, 'Maui Forever,' sitting on a drum table next to the digital frame. Then the double underline of the First Bass's assertion, 'You're giving them the map for the road to Hana.' And finally, the reference to Charles and Anne Lindbergh in *McGill*."

"And what do the Lindberghs have to do with Maui?" I asked.

"I read an article in the *Smithsonian* last summer," Jennifer replied. "They built a retreat there on a five-acre estate down a winding road in Kipahulu. It's some ten miles southwest, on the far side of Hana."

I smiled and said, "So it looks like we have to prioritize. Will it be Washington or Hana? How do you want to choose our first destination?"

She laughed aloud. "How about a coin flip with the winner choosing our first stop?"

"Fine by me," I said. "Here's a quarter."

Jennifer looked away and mumbled, "Heads, I win. Tails, you lose." She quickly flipped the coin and announced, "Tails it is. You lose!" She gave me a teasing poke in the side.

I laughed and said, "Okay, have it your way. Spending Christmas on an unproductive trip to paradise can't be all bad."

Three days later we were touching down at Kahului Airport, picking up our rental car, and checking into our boutique hotel several miles from the terminal. The following morning we rose before dawn and headed over to the "Highway to Heaven." After a death-defying, picturesque journey of six hundred hairpin curves; slick, one-lane roads; blind turns; distracting views; and unprotected cliffs with wrecked cars strewn about thousands of feet below us, we reached the end of the world, Hana Town, a small village tucked in among banyan trees and the red-orange blossoms of African tulips.

With Sam's photo in hand we made unsuccessful stops at the Hasegawa General Store, the cultural center, and the Wananalua Congregational Church. After the reverend's wife explained she and her husband had ministered to the congregation going on fifteen years and had never seen anyone like Sam accompanying a woman in a wheelchair either at the church or anywhere else around the small town, I glanced over at Jennifer, smiled smugly, and said, "Well, after the holidays, I guess it's on to Washington."

She shook her head and said, "No, not so fast. We need to make one or two more stops before I'm ready to throw in the towel."

"So where are we headed now that we've reached the end of the inhabited world?"

She whispered, "To Kipahulu and perhaps on to Kaupo, just beyond the end of the world on the other side of sadness."

After a second unsuccessful stop, this time in Kipahulu, we headed southwest along the rugged coastline to Jennifer's last gasp, the tiny fishing village of Kaupo. We pulled up in front of the general store and eased in beside several horses tied to a hitching post. We climbed the steps and entered this one-story cabin with corrugated roof and salt-soaked boards sporting few hints of its original dark-green paint. The interior beyond the red and white BEER– WINE– SAKÉ sign was in fact more museum than store. The shelves were lined with a unique collection of antique bottles, clocks, cameras, and radios. The pièces de résistance included a radio made from a cookie sheet and a clock crafted from the dashboard of a mid-twentieth-century roadster.

We approached the manager with Sam's photo in hand. After introducing ourselves and explaining our mission, a voice behind us eased into the conversation. "She said you would come," the voice said. Jennifer and I glanced at each other in astonishment as we wheeled around and asked simultaneously, "What did you say?"

A muscular native Hawaiian in his forties approached and repeated his claim: "She said you would come. Sam said you would come." He extended his hand and introduced himself. "I'm David Kamakau, former caretaker of the cottage and grounds. You can call me Kami. That's what Sam and all my friends call me."

I couldn't hold back any longer. I interrupted, "You mean Sam is here? Where is she? Is Marta with her?"

He pointed to the saddlebags draped around his neck and answered, "Let me settle up for my goods here, and then we'll head on out to the house where we can speak privately."

After paying for his things, he joined us in the parking lot, where he unhitched one of the horses and swung up into the saddle. He pointed back up the road to the east and shouted, "Follow me. The turnoff is just up there an eighth of a mile on the left."

We fell in behind Kami, zigzagged around the same batch of potholes we had just negotiated ten minutes earlier, and then turned left onto a rugged jeep trail. Following several twists and bends, Kami signaled a right-hand turn, which led us up a narrow path to a two-story A-frame partially hidden behind tall shrubs and sandalwood. He hitched his horse near the front door and gestured broadly, signaling for us to get out of the car and follow him into the house.

"Please come in and make yourselves at home," he said warmly. "Why don't you take a seat on the futon there while I whip us up a quick pitcher of pineapple iced tea."

As he disappeared around the corner into the kitchen, I leaned over to Jennifer and whispered, "Looks like we're working on two sets of clocks here. You and I are here on a mission, hell-bent to get answers, and he's in there dallying about making tea and holding all the cards close to the vest."

Jennifer patted me on the forearm and said, "Patience, Kyle. We're almost home now. We're almost home."

Several minutes later Kami returned with the tea and said, "How about a toast?"

We nodded, stood up, and raised our drinks as our host declared, "To Sam and Marta!"

Jennifer and I responded in unison, "To Sam and Marta!"

Kami took several long draughts of his tea and said, "If you're okay with it, I suppose the best way to go at this is to go back a few years so I won't forget anything."

"Whatever's best for you, Kami," Jennifer encouraged him.

He nodded, paused briefly to collect his thoughts, and then surprised us by beginning with his own biography. "I was born in Kipahulu. Went up through high school in Hana. Stayed there with an aunt during the school year. A blessing with eight brothers and sisters at home. After four years in the navy, I came home and got a job crushing rock for a road crew. I figured two years of that was enough, so I hitched on as a paniolo with the ranch out here. Little bit of everything. Still some pick and shovel work but mostly running the herds from one pasture to the next. Some thousand head at a time! I had been at that for some six or so years when the priest took me aside and told me a couple of ladies had moved into the old Mawae place and were in desperate need of a caretaker for the grounds, the house, and for one of the ladies who was in the late stages of ALS—you know, Lou Gehrig's disease. Well, I took his suggestion and rode out here to the house. I immediately saw the need and signed on to help them out. Sad thing about that. Caring for Marta was a short-term job. She was really sick when she arrived and got progressively worse very quickly. A couple bouts of pneumonia, an embolism, and then her heart gave out." He shook his head while pausing to revisit the suffering.

I eased in to his monologue empathetically. "Those must have been difficult times for you, Kami. Can you tell me, how did Sam react to Marta's illness and death?"

Kami shook his head again and said, "She didn't take to it well at all. You see, Sam put on a brave face throughout those last weeks and months. I guess to keep Marta's spirits up. But once we had had the cremation and funeral, it seemed the life just began to bleed out of her, too. I couldn't get her motivated to do anything again—tending her orchids, hiking the trails up the slope to Haleakala. Hard to get her to get out of bed or eat anything. I finally got so concerned I rode up to Kipahulu to fetch my younger sister. You see, she's a nurse." He paused, shook his head for a third time, and mumbled, "But by the time we got back, she was gone."

"Left the house?" Jennifer whispered.

"No, nothing like that. When my sister and I got back here, we went upstairs to her bedroom and discovered a rope stretching from the center beam out the raised window. We didn't have to look. We just knew. So we went downstairs, and my sister called the state police."

I whispered to myself, "Life imitating art, Bianca."

"So what happened next?" Jennifer asked.

Kami shrugged and said, "Well, after the cremation we had a private funeral for her. I mean my family and me. And then we read the will she had left in the desk drawer over there. I'll show it to you later when we get up. It was short and to the point. She listed only two possessions." He paused, slowly waved his arms, and said, "The house and land, which she graciously willed to me, and then there were some manuscripts and papers, which she left for you, Kyle."

I glanced over at Jennifer and began tearing up with conflicting emotions. On the one hand I was heartbroken my sister had taken her own life, but on the other hand I was encouraged knowing that Jennifer and I had been on the right track all along. Sam had entrusted her life's work to my keeping. I took a deep breath to compose myself and asked, "So where are Sam and Marta buried, Kami? Jennifer and I would like to visit the grave site."

He looked up, pointed toward the ceiling, and responded, "Ah, they're not resting in any cemetery, Kyle. As Sam said time and time again during her last months, 'When I die, our urns are to remain upstairs on the dresser in the bedroom until Kyle comes a-calling. And then he and only he is to unseal the envelope that I've placed in the middle dresser drawer.'" Kami paused and added, "And you'll see, Kyle, the envelope's still there after all these years. Sealed. Waiting for you to open it. You ready to go upstairs?"

I nodded and stood up. "Yes, it's way past time for a reunion with my sister. Come on, Jenn."

We climbed the narrow steps and entered Sam's old bedroom where she lived, suffered, and died. To our left, on the seven-drawer rattan dresser, we found the two ceramic cremation urns fired in mixtures of blue, silver, copper, and gray. Brushed-gold pendants hung from the necks of the urns, the one on the left inscribed simply with "Marta" and the one on the right with "Sam." Kami, Jennifer, and I moved to the dresser, bowed our heads, and honored the lovers each in our own way.

I then opened the middle drawer; and as I pulled out the yellowing envelope, Kami asked, "Do you want to take the letter downstairs where it's more comfortable and you'll have more light?"

I shook my head and said, "No. I think I'd just like to sit up here on the edge of the bed and read it." As I began tearing the envelope open, my hands shook with nerves. Jennifer and Kami turned and started walking toward the door. I looked up and said, "No, no, it's okay. Please stay. We're all kind of in this together."

13

I TOOK A DEEP BREATH, pulled Sam's letter from the envelope, and began reading:

> *Forgive me, Son, for I have sinned. I was very young, sixteen at the time. And it was equal parts passion and curiosity. While their religion required me to carry you to term, the parents and I struck a deal where you would stay with them and I would attend college and pursue my career. But Kyle, let me be clear. I had every intention of returning for you once I had finished the degree and established myself professionally.*
>
> *But as time and distance blunted purpose, I reasoned you were better off with their love and support than with my unpredictability and hand-to-mouth existence. And besides, you had grown old enough now where an unsettling explanation would be due. So why turn your young world upside down? Why rip you away from your*

reality? But one thing I swore upon your life for sure, I would never again allow my life's work to interfere with my love.

But Beckett had it right, didn't he? Try again. Fail again. Fail better. I loved Marta. I loved her more deeply than I had ever loved before. I wouldn't have intentionally harmed her for the world. She had been stable for some time, and I believed the trip to the States would do her some good. And even if she became ill while I was conducting the seminar, she would be in good hands. After all, the Lynches still held sway at McGill General.

Yet despite the expert emergency care, the doctors and Marta knew she only had a few weeks or months to live. The arc depended on her willingness to fight and how quickly the thumb moved away along the balance beam. So what next then? Where to? An easy decision—reprise the memories of Maui. But the gods have a way, don't they, Kyle? No, they would have none of that. So we arrived just in time for her last weeks (not hours) of suffering.

Marta's death and my guilt beat me to my knees. Kept beating me down until I no longer had the will to rise and continue the fight. Which brings me now full circle to you, Son, and to a mother's

prayer for forgiveness and of hope that you will
mingle our ashes at Puu ʻO Pele and then continue
westward on your winding way finishing the work
I had so fearlessly begun.

After reading the closing lines, I moved over to the dresser, handed Jennifer the letter, and said, "Looks like we still have some work to do, Jenn, but the rest will practically write itself. You'll see." I then turned and bit my lip until it bled.

14

VERY EARLY THE NEXT morning the five of us took a
right out of Kami's driveway back onto the dirt road, which
would thread its way up through Kaupo Gap toward our first
overnight at the Paliku Cabin inside the Haleakala crater.
The first part of our strenuous eight-mile, six-thousand-foot
climb took us on a searing, dusty trek through Kaupo Ranch
where we stopped briefly to watch Kami's old paniolo bud-
dies run five hundred head of white-faced angus eastward
toward a fresh alpine grassland.

For the second half of our all-day journey, we traded the
rutted jeep trail, blistered feet, and an intense tropical sun for
steep switchbacks, twisted ankles, and the cool, wet shade of
a koa cloud forest. We arrived at the cabin near sunset. Our
one-story, two-room sanctuary was nestled at the base of
steep, ocher-tinged cliffs and surrounded by a lush jungle of
ferns, flowering plants, and tropical trees. Just to the right of
our redwood cabin was an unoccupied ranger station and
stable, where a dozen or so friendly nene wandered about
pecking at the thick turf.

Our two-room cabin was composed of a kitchen and a modest great room for dining, sleeping, and sharing stories. While the center of the space featured a long table and benches carved with the fleeting biographies of the living and the dead, the corners were reserved for padded bunks in stacks of three. Jennifer shivered, crossing her arms and rubbing her hands against her shoulders. "It sure gets chilly up here once the sun sets behind the crater wall."

Kami smiled, leaned his backpack and poles against a stack of bunks, and responded hospitably, "Your wish, my dear, is my command."

While he built a roaring fire in the cast-iron kitchen stove, I rustled up a feast of crystallized eggs and fried spam on a propane burner. After dinner, we retreated to our respective corners for some personal time—to read, reflect, or post entries in a private journal. But Pele would have none of that. The ancient goddess demanded attention first with booming thunder and then with crackling light animating the ghostly cinder cones below.

The following morning I awoke at sunrise to the sound of Kami rearranging his backpack and Jennifer boiling water for some strong black breakfast tea. I swung my legs around off the bed and stumbled over to the table, where I discovered Jennifer had already fixed "breakfast," piling a generous stack of chocolate chip oatmeal cookies on a paper plate. Kami approached the table and said with a laugh, "I was hoping to make off with all the stash before you woke up."

I raised my head out of my hands, ignoring his banter. "You heading out already?"

"Yeah. I want to get an early start, miss the peak heat of the day down on the ranch."

"I know what you mean. Unbelievable. It was hotter than hell down there yesterday only days away from Christmas!" I paused to end the chitchat and couched nailing down the pickup plans in a word of thanks. "Say, Kami, Jenn and I sure appreciate your offer to drive the rental around to the western slope and meet us at the trailhead tomorrow."

He smiled and replied, "No problem, man. I'll be up top at the crack of dawn watching the sunrise. It just never grows old. And then I'll get some shuteye in the car until you guys make it up to the top sometime near noon."

"Well, we want you to know how much we appreciate it."

"Hey, what goes around comes around. We'll just say next time it'll be on the two of you. How's that?"

"You've got a deal!" Jennifer said as she entered the room with a pot of steaming tea.

Kami moved over to his bunk, swung his pack up onto his shoulders, and announced, "Well, I'm going to be getting out of here now."

We followed him outside and escorted him a hundred yards or so back down the Kaupo Gap trail. When we reached the edge of the forest, we stopped, gave him a big hug, and watched him disappear into the heavy, wet mist.

After finishing off the tea and cookies, Jennifer and I packed up our things and headed west on the terminal segment of the Halemauu Trail. Our mission today, on this singular winter solstice, was to fulfill a mother's dream. We hiked the first mile and a half through drenched 'Ohi'a groves flowering in deep reds and yellows before reaching a landscape of polar opposites—a stark, gray, sterile desert dotted with pits, caves, and giant lunar-like cinder cones.

But then just ahead on the left we discovered our fire and brimstone destination—the most striking cinder cone of all, the Puu 'O Pele, or Pele's Paint Pot, with its vibrant oranges, rusts, browns, and creams flowing down the sensuous curving sides onto the winding trail. We walked over to the base of the cone, dug a shallow trench with our hands, and mingled the lovers' remains in a final everlasting embrace.

Following a few brief words of forgiveness and commitment, we consulted a map to guide us to a trail headed southeast toward our next overnight at the Kapalaoa Cabin.

We had heard it was a rare occurrence, but we soon realized we would have the cabin all to ourselves that night. And while we splurged on a final dinner of freeze-dried beef stroganoff and strawberries, Jennifer asked, "Why do you think Sam chose to come here in the first place? The beauty of the island? The isolation? The solitude?"

I nodded and replied, "I suspect a little bit of all three, but I would like to think it also had something to do with the legend."

"The legend?"

"Of the demigod, Maui, performing two of his greatest feats here in the crater—battling the gods and lifting the sky. That's what I think she was doing in the narrative, following Maui's lead. Battling the gods and trying to lift the skies."

"And why the Puu 'O Pele as a resting place for the two of them?"

"If I had to guess… Remember what she wrote about Master Hudson in *Warfield*? She said, 'He mounted his one-room stage and spoke to us in pictures.' So I would like to imagine she chose the Paint Pot because she viewed herself and Marta as artists who metaphorically painted their works with words instead of oils."

Jennifer looked down, twirled the stroganoff with her fork, and asked, "You okay with something a bit more personal? I mean after suffering the shock."

"It's okay, Jenn. What you got?"

"The motif. It troubled me a lot from the outset."

"Which one?"

"Mr. Jaffe's 'appearance and reality' motif. It threw me for a real loop. I just couldn't wrap my head around it. Get it to fit. Integrate it with the others, with the existential motifs."

I nodded again. "I know what you mean. I didn't say anything at the time, but it bothered me too. I was hoping that somewhere, somehow an inspiration would come along and connect the dots. And boy did it ever! And from the least likely of places, too."

Jennifer shook her head. "And ironically, you'd now have to say 'appearance and reality' is right up there with 'loss' and 'existentialism.'"

"Especially as the motif applies to the biographical underpinning of her inspiration. But you know, Jenn, it was sitting there all along right under our noses, and we just didn't see it."

"What do you mean?"

"Well, the one thing she danced around and didn't talk about during that first lecture after Thanksgiving was Bianca's trip back to Europe purportedly for an extended tour promoting her latest volume of poetry. Turned out Bianca was pregnant, stayed at the quinta until after the birth, and then left Danielle behind with the grandparents. That's as close as she ever came to revealing a genuine biographical truth. Bianca even describes the pressures, the guilt of leaving her baby behind in Portugal. That's when the poetess began showing the first signs of instability."

Jennifer extended her arms across the table and held my hands in hers. After a long, reflective pause I began envisioning a quick shower out back and then a cozy, intimate night sharing a bunk. But Jennifer had other ideas. She said, "How about we get a real early start."

"What time you have in mind?"

"As soon as we can clean up the cabin and gather up our things. It's close to a full moon tonight, and we could make the summit in time to share a spectacular sunrise with Kami."

I smiled, gazed into her eyes, and said, "You're right, Jenn. That's a great idea. It's time to put Sam's—ah, Mom's—long narrative to bed. There's no better way to end her story than with a Haleakala sunrise."

So on the third day a little past midnight we finished packing and exited the cabin to begin the demanding ascent. I paused, gazed out toward the moonlit cliffs, and whispered, "By the rivers of Babylon, there we sat down, yea, we wept, when we remembered Zion." And after passing several sentries of silversword, we stepped out onto the Sliding Sands Trail and moved westward beneath their timeless tiara of ten thousand stars.

EPILOGUE:

SUNRISE

"What do you see there?"

"I see beauty."